THE DEAD MAN

Even as I walked up to the open door, I had an uneasy feeling that I was going to find something out of order. I called out again, and still getting no answer, I came close enough to peek in.

I saw a man's foot—or rather, a man's shoe pointing upward from the floor. Whoever was wearing that shoe had a thick ankle covered with a grey wool sock, and he wore common drab pants just like the ones Mr. Earlywine had been wearing the day before. Then I saw the other foot and leg, and I was pretty sure it was Mr. Earlywine lying on the floor. I dropped the reins on the ground and stepped into the house.

It was Mr. Earlywine, all right, lying flat on his back with his belly sticking up. His dull eyes and dark mouth were open, and I could tell he wasn't going to move again under his own power. He hadn't shaved since I had seen him last, and a fly was crawling across the stubble on his cheek toward the corner of his mouth. It looked as if there was a larger fly on his forehead, and then I saw that it was a bullet hole….

Other *Leisure* books by John D. Nesbitt:

WEST OF ROCK RIVER
RED WIND CROSSING
BLACK HAT BUTTE
FOR THE NORDEN BOYS
MAN FROM WOLF RIVER
NORTH OF CHEYENNE
COYOTE TRAIL
WILD ROSE OF RUBY CANYON
BLACK DIAMOND RENDEZVOUS
ONE-EYED COWBOY WILD

RANCHO ALEGRE

JOHN D. NESBITT

LEISURE BOOKS  NEW YORK CITY

For Sonny Boy and Partner

A LEISURE BOOK®

July 2005

Published by

Dorchester Publishing Co., Inc.
200 Madison Avenue
New York, NY 10016

ISBN 0-8439-5540-6

Printed in the United States of America.

RANCHO ALEGRE

Chapter One

Rancho Alegre means "happy ranch." I had never heard of the place before, and I had no idea I was headed there the day I went to see Mr. Earlywine. He had no such idea, either, I'm sure. He wanted me to go to Pueblo, in southern Colorado, but I wasn't all that taken by his idea. I didn't think I was going anywhere, but as I would find out later, I was going to Rancho Alegre.

It all started one day in late summer when I was sitting in my camp at the river, upstream from Red Wind Crossing. I was trying to make a halter out of a rope, and it was giving me trouble. To do work like that, a fellow needs to have it in him to do things right, to be precise, and to be willing to untie the knots and draw them finer. I'm not so good at tending to small details like that, but I knew I needed the practice and I didn't have anything else to do, so I was trying my patience with twenty feet of three-eighths-inch hemp rope. What I would have liked was to be sitting in the Jack-Deuce, drinking a mug of cold beer and listening to stories. But I knew I needed to stay out of those places at least until later in the day, so I was making myself stick to the task. Nevertheless, when a lean stranger rode up and told me a man named Mr. Earlywine wanted to see me about some possible work, I was willing to set my project aside and go get my horse ready.

The lean man rode off after telling me where to find Mr. Earlywine, and I didn't see him again. I tidied up my camp, fetched and saddled my horse, and stopped to think. I had the feeling that someone else was going to want to come and visit me, and I couldn't see a way to leave a note, so I took some sticks of firewood and laid out an arrow pointing toward town. I've had that kind of feeling before, but the way it usually runs for me, I can expect or rather hope that some pretty girl will show up, but instead I get a snaggletoothed washerwoman telling me I owe her money, or a down-at-the-heels saddle tramp asking if he can roll out his blankets for the night. Nevertheless, I left the note and climbed onto my horse. As I rode out of my camp, I glanced at the arrow made of sticks, and I wondered if it would make as much sense to a visitor as it did to me.

The town of Monetta wasn't very large, but there were a lot of people I didn't know. For one thing, the white folks lived on one side of the river while the Mexicans lived on the other, and I had friends on both sides. Whenever I came to town, I spent a little time on each side and then went back out to the ranch country. So it didn't surprise me to learn for the first time that there was a man named Mr. Earlywine in the town, and it didn't seem odd that someone would send for me to do some work. All Mr. Earlywine, or anyone like him, had to do was ask around for someone who was out of work, and sooner or later one of the loafers about town would point him in my direction.

What had my curiosity, though, was the question of what Mr. Earlywine might want me to do.

Once, when I was growing up on the farm, a fellow named Mr. Benson, who lived in a big house in town, needed a boy to do some work. It seemed like a good opportunity, not only to earn a little money of my own but also to get away from home for a while, so I rode into town, hoping he didn't want me to pluck chickens. I don't like the smell of chicken feathers in hot water. It turned out he wanted me to wash his dog, which was a big St. Bernard, old and drooling with matted hair. It was the first job I was offered and the first one I turned down, and ever since then it's served as sort of a model, reminding me that I don't have to take every job that comes my way. Of course, there have been some jobs I took and would have been better off without, and that was another thing I was trying to stay away from.

I found Mr. Earlywine's place where the lean messenger had told me to look, on a back street, the house facing west with empty lots all around it. It was a common-looking building, wide and low with a stucco exterior. It had no porch or shade trees on the west side, and the tan coloring of the stucco had a baked look in the summer sun.

As my horse's hooves sounded on the hard, dry ground of the front yard, a bulky man appeared at the left side of the house.

"Are you Jimmy Clevis?" he asked.

"I sure am." I swung down from my horse.

"Well, I'm Milton Earlywine. Why don't you come around back, where we can sit in the shade."

He held out his hand, and I shook it. Before I got a good look at him, he turned and led me around the house. The back yard was no more fixed up than the front, though it had a henhouse with no chickens and a low coal or wood shed with weeds all around it. At least there wasn't a big slobbering dog on the end of a chain, although it wouldn't have been out of place. My general impression was that the house and yard had gone untended for a while and that Mr. Earlywine hadn't lived there very long.

I tied my horse to a post that stood alone in the full sun, and then I went to sit in the shade of the house, where Mr. Earlywine had two cane-back chairs set on the dry ground. I didn't see a table, or glasses, or anything else promising, but I took off my hat all the same as I sat down.

I got a better look at him now. I placed him somewhere in middle age, around fifty or so. His face and body had filled out, and he didn't look as if he had done much physical labor. He wasn't neat like a merchant on Main Street, either. He had the casual upkeep of a man who shaved every two or three days, bathed once a week, and changed his clothes when they got dirty. The clothes he wore were loose-fitting and common, not smudged or frayed from work. For his age he had a good head of hair, parted on the left and combed back on top, gray like the stubble of his beard. Tiny broken veins showed on his upper cheeks and across his nose, and a second chin was holding up the first one, which didn't look as if it had been all that firm to begin with.

Leaning back in his chair and tipping to his left, he took a cigar from his waistcoat pocket. He bit off one end and spit it away, took his time to light the other end, and then turned his gaze on me. He had steady brown eyes, and he seemed to pride himself in giving a shrewd look.

"They tell me you're a good hand, Clevis."

"I suppose it depends on what kind of work. I've done different kinds."

"So have I." He held his cigar out to get a sideways view of it, then looked back at me. "I was in the cooperage business for several years, in the ice business for a few, and more lately was in the line of supplying dry goods to mining camps."

"Oh. Blankets and clothing and candles and such?"

He sniffed. "Something like that. But I sold that business, just like the other two, and I'm thinkin' about what I want to go into next."

"I see." Actually, I didn't. If he was out of a line of work, it was hard for me to imagine what he wanted me to do.

"There's always another opportunity, just waitin' to be found."

"I'm sure."

"But that's not what we sat down to talk about."

"That's all right, too."

"What I want is for you to do a piece of work for me, unrelated to any of my past or future business enterprises."

"I see. You mean a specific job, not just day-in and day-out delivery of ice or candles."

"That's right. A task. When I asked around, I heard that you were out of work and might be the kind of man to do the job I have in mind."

"Well, like I said earlier, it depends on what kind."

"I'll try to give you an idea, and you can judge for yourself." He took a long puff on the cigar and held it out as if to inspect the ash. Then he gave me the knowing look again. "Someone took something from me, and I'd like to get it back."

"Oh. What did they steal?"

Mr. Earlywine frowned. "It's hard to come right out and say it was stolen. If I could call it that, I could just go to the sheriff. But we'll put it in these terms, that someone got off with something that was mine. This person is a chiseler and an opportunist, or to put it more broadly, a son of a bitch. He knows me and had access to this thing, and he took it."

"But you just can't call it a theft."

"I'm not as interested in that as I am in getting the thing back."

I was imagining something small and valuable, like a ring or a watch. It might be a document, but he called it a thing, which made me think more along the lines of some piece of portable property that had value. I also wondered if he was being so discreet because the thing might have come into his possession in some questionable way. Whatever the case, he seemed to like to keep his information wrapped up. I decided to play the guessing game with him a little further. "Is it something, then, that you'd like me to go get and bring back?"

"That's right."

"And do you have some idea of where it is?"

"I have a pretty good idea it's in Pueblo."

"The town of Pueblo, down south of Colorado Springs."

"Yes."

"Huh." I pictured a long trail going south. "Then I don't suppose this thing is very big, if you want me to bring it all the way back from there."

"It's not small, and it's not big."

I felt that instead of playing I was being played with, so I said, "Could I venture to ask what it is?"

He answered me with a straight, direct gaze. "It's a saddle, Clevis."

"Oh." I formed an image of a typical saddle, smooth brown leather and not quite new anymore. "Is there anything unusual about it?"

"Not really. Not in its appearance, anyway." He put the cigar in his mouth.

"But I would guess it has some importance, other than just its value as a saddle."

He gave me an approving look as he drew on the cigar. Then he blew out the smoke and said, "Yes, it's something that someone else would like to have, and not just to ride or sell." He settled back in his chair.

"Well, I'll tell you, Mr. Earlywine. If I had some idea of why it had that value, I could decide whether it was something I would want to try to get back for you."

He lifted his head and turned it a few degrees to one side, and the wrinkles in his neck reminded me of a turtle. "It has a piece of information hidden in it."

"Oh."

"There are some initials engraved on it somewhere, not in plain sight."

"And those initials are of interest to someone, I suppose." I thought I was starting to get the idea, and I felt pleased with myself for figuring things out.

He didn't answer me directly. "I'll tell you, they can change the stirrups, the conchos, the rosettes, the strings, and so forth, but they can't change the thing they don't know about."

"You mean, they don't know where it is."

"Exactly. They don't know where it's embedded." He lifted his chins.

I was beginning to think of a word that referred to one person holding information over another. It was not a very nice word, and I began to feel less pleased with myself.

He must have sensed my hesitation. In a confidential tone he said, "If you accept the job, I'll tell you what the letters are and where they're hidden. Right now I can tell you that they're not the initials of the person who took the saddle, and that person doesn't know where the information is concealed."

"He just knows that the saddle has something that allows one person to hold something over someone else."

"That puts it rather clearly without going into detail."

I sat back in my chair. "I don't know. It sounds like there might be some trouble."

He gave me a look of assurance through the haze of cigar smoke. "From what I understand, you can take care of yourself."

I had been through a set of scrapes not too long before that, and I imagined he had heard about it. "Yeah," I answered. "Sometimes a fellow has to. But if trouble has a tendency to come his way, he doesn't like to borrow any more."

Mr. Earlywine took what seemed like an impatient heave of breath. "There doesn't have to be any trouble. It's just a matter of recovering something that doesn't belong to the party that has it. The way I see it, when you decide you want to get something back, you put your mind to it and you don't let anyone keep you from doing it."

I put on a thoughtful look, and he left me alone for a

moment as I mulled it over. It seemed as if this fellow Earlywine or the person who took the saddle, or both, had something to hold over someone else. The word for it came back to me again, and I had to draw a line for myself to decide whether taking this job would make me some kind of a helper or whether I could separate myself from that and just do the part that was my job. Then there was the idea of the saddle being stolen, even though Mr. Earlywine said it wasn't really a theft. To me it seemed like one, and I didn't like the idea of coming into contact with thieves, if I wasn't already there. I'd had enough of their company in the past and was trying to do without it. If a person has ever had that inclination, he knows that it's not quite as easy to swear off as a normal habit, like chewing stringy tobacco. It's more like kissing your cousin, which I haven't done but I've done things similar.

"I don't know," I said. "Have you considered anyone else?"

"I've talked to a couple of these greasers, but I don't like their way of doing things."

I didn't know what he meant by that, and I didn't care for his tone, but I thought it was pretty likely they wouldn't care for him either if he classed them that way. I didn't say anything. I waited for him to speak again, which he did after a long moment.

"It's worth a hundred dollars to me," he said. "Sixty to begin with, and forty when you get back. That's anywhere from two to three months' pay at cowhand wages, and you could get it done in a little over a week if you went about it right."

"I don't know."

"You don't have to decide right now. Why don't you take a day or two to think about it?" He lifted his cigar to his mouth and gave me a steady look as he took a puff.

"I could do that." I stood up and put my hat on my head, as a way of getting ready to go.

He pushed himself up and held out his hand. "Give it a thought. I think you're the man to do it." After a firm handshake and another assuring look, he sat down and let me go.

I walked into the sunlight and untied my horse from the post. He was a tall horse with a long neck, which made for short reins on the outfit I had. I took care not to drop the reins as I poked my toe up into the stirrup and pulled myself aboard. I turned and nodded to Mr. Earlywine, who sat in the shade puffing on his cigar. He made a small wave of good-bye with his free hand.

As I rode out of town, I resisted two temptations. One was to go to the Jack-Deuce, and the other was to go see a girl I knew. Staying away from the saloon called for some willpower, sort of a battle of either-or, even though I already had the rule laid out for myself. Not going to see the girl was a problem of a different order. I was tempted, but not because I felt a lure or a beckoning, as I might say in the case of the saloon. With the girl, I wasn't sure how welcome I was. I could remember Magdalena, her eyes shining, as she told me I should throw a little to the wind, enjoy myself. But she had told me that in order to help me get over a blondie girl, as I had heard it put, and I didn't know if she meant I should try enjoying things with her. I had to admit that I was afraid to try very much with Magdalena because I was afraid to fail. I thought she could rub out anything I thought I had going with the blondie girl, but I felt I needed to let that stuff settle a little more on its own.

In addition to all of that, I wanted a while alone to mull over Mr. Earlywine's proposal, even though I didn't expect to take him up on it. As I rode back to my camp, I didn't feel very convinced. It seemed like a lot of trouble over a saddle I didn't care enough about. There had been a time when I might have lifted a saddle myself, for less personal reasons, so I understood that part of it, but there seemed to be a lot more than simple property caught up in this one.

Back at camp I saw the stick arrow on the ground as I had left it. It seemed to be pointing toward Mr. Earlywine, whose image I could still see as he sat in a haze of cigar smoke. I swung down, and with my boot I dragged the sticks into a little pile of firewood. I stripped the horse and put him out to graze. Then, with nothing else to do, I went back to working on the rope halter.

From where I sat, I could see my saddle when I looked up from my work. I had set it on a log to keep it from picking up sand, and as I saw it, it made me think. I try to take care of the few belongings I have, but sometimes it's still hard to do things right. Like punching holes in leather. I could see my latigo and the hole I had made with my pocketknife when I got the bigger horse. A real leather worker or saddle maker would never do that. He would say, tie it in a necktie knot until you could get a leather punch to do it right. Some lessons I had learned, like not to oil a latigo. All it took was one chewing-out, years earlier, by an old codger, and I learned not to do it. But other habits seemed to come back, and then when the deed is done, it stays around to remind a fellow what kind of a man has a poor way of doing things.

I couldn't change having grown up poor, and that in itself didn't cause me any feelings of shame. But the things I did, and the way I did them—I knew I needed to work on some of them. So I paid close attention to the hemp rope, keeping the strands as close and even as I could, and drawing the knots tight. Every once in a while I looked up to relax my sight, and I would catch another glance of my saddle. In addition to making me think of my own habits, it made me think of Mr. Earlywine's saddle. I wondered what information it might have, as he said, concealed, and what secrets might be linked to it. Then I put it out of my mind and went back to my strands and knots.

Chapter Two

The shadows of morning were drawing back from the middle of the street when I rode down the main thoroughfare of Monetta. After sleeping on Mr. Earlywine's offer, I thought I might ask around before I turned him down. I was pretty well settled that I didn't want to take the job, but I had time to find out if there was anything else I should know.

I tied my horse to the hitch rack in front of the Crest Café and went inside. I was looking for Tom, or Tome as the Mexicans pronounced his name, so that it rhymed with "home." I knew I could find him sometimes in the café in the morning and usually in the Jack-Deuce in the afternoon. Since I hadn't thought to look him up the day before when I was being so diligent about staying away from the saloon, I decided to try the café this morning. Luck was on my side, it seemed, as he was sitting by himself at a table along the wall. I picked him out by his gray hair and Vandyke beard. He had on his glasses, as usual, and was reading a Denver newspaper that I supposed was a few days old but the newest one in town. His pipe sat on the table next to his coffee cup, along with a little tamping tool that he used when he had the pipe going. He looked up from his reading, raised his eyebrows, and motioned for me to take a seat.

"Well, young Galahad, what wind blows you this way on such a fine morning?"

"No wind," I said as I sat down. "Everything's calm."

"Huh. A smooth sea never made a skilled mariner. I hate to see you have things so easy, when you should be out there suffering away your youth."

"I try."

He folded the paper and set it aside, then wiped the palm of his hand downward on his beard. "I know. And I trust you to get into some more misery just as soon as you can manage it."

"I might have a chance right now, though I think I'll pass it up."

His large head made a quarter turn, and I could see his scalp through the thin hair. "Oh, what's that?"

"A fellow with the last name of Earlywine offered me a job. He lives here in town."

Tome shook his head. "Haven't heard of him."

"Well, he wants someone to go all the way to Pueblo to bring back a saddle that another person took from him. And he doesn't want to go to the law with it, because he says it wasn't exactly stolen. Sounds like too much trouble to me."

"I'd say. If he can't do it himself and he can't go to the law, there's a good chance there's trouble in it."

"That's sort of the way I saw it. I haven't given him my answer yet, but I think I'll turn it down. It does pay a little bit, though, and I need to find something before long."

Tome pointed at me with his pipe stem. "I'll tell you, if you want to run an errand for someone, I might know of a possibility." He lowered his voice and gave me a confidential look. "I know a man here in town who's looking for a discreet party to do a bit of detective kind of work. He wants to find someone he lost track of."

"Just find them?"

Tome gave a shrug. "He could tell you more, but I don't think he's looking to have any grievances redressed or anything like that. He just wants to find a long-lost—well, I shouldn't say any more. But you can tell him I recommended you. I think he expected to get someone who was in that line of work already, and I don't think he was expecting to find anyone around here, but it wouldn't hurt to ask."

"Sounds worth it to me. What's his name?"

Tome lowered his voice again. "Tull. Lawrence Tull."

I shook my head. "I don't know him."

"I think he's honest enough, but you can judge for yourself. At the very least, he'd be good for his money, and it doesn't sound like dangerous work."

"I suppose so. Where's he live?"

"About four blocks from here. Two blocks west and then two blocks over to the right. It's a big house with green shutters. Stone foundation, mansard roof, little dormer windows. Big porch."

"I think I know the place. I just didn't know what kind of people lived there."

"Good people. We wouldn't have any other kind in our town."

"Right."

"Actually, I do think he's rather decent. And like I said,

the danger of knives and bullets would be pretty low." He cocked his head. "Of course, with you, there's no tellin'. You see a girl walkin' down the street, and the next thing anyone knows, you have to shoot your way out of a whorehouse."

"That was just a mistake. I don't get into things like that every day."

"Well, if you're goin' to go around those places, just go to the ones where you can go in and out of the front door."

"I'll remember that."

"The back door is for the chambermaid and for anyone the management wants to keep out of public view."

"Mucky-mucks?"

"Them, and the other extreme." Tome paused, as if he wasn't sure whether to say more, and then he went on. "Not that a black man or a yellow man has any different kind of equipment, as any of those girls could tell you, but some white men don't like to know about it, if they're goin' to be in there next."

"Oh."

"Just a bit of sage advice from your uncle as you venture out into the world. Go through the front door. And if they don't like you there—well, go somewhere else."

"I'll bear it in mind. And thanks for the tip on this job."

He turned down the corners of his mouth. "No tellin' what he'll say, but no harm in askin'. And if it turns out to be an honest job for you, it won't be the worst thing that ever happened."

"Thanks." That was one thing I always appreciated about Tome. He didn't mince his words.

* * *

I found the Tull house without any problem. From a block away, the two little attic windows looked like arched eyebrows on a demon, but as I got closer the place took on a respectable air. The stone foundation, the long porch, and the green shutters all gave an impression of stability. People who took the trouble to keep the shutters painted and the porch level seemed to be the kind who kept up standards for the rest of us. And they indeed were the kind who had work for some of the other half, which is where I put myself. I tied my horse to the ring of the hitching post and walked between two little spruce trees to reach the porch. Feeling confident with Tome's recommendation, I walked up the steps and used the brass knocker to rap on the door.

A long moment later, the door opened and I was looking at a younger man than I expected. He might have been a couple of years older than I was, but he had a level of self-assurance that went along with living in a house like that. He was healthy and athletic-looking, very neat and trimmed with a shiny watch chain and a blond mustache. He had quick blue eyes that seemed to take in my horse and come back to me in a flicker.

"Are you Mr. Tull?" I asked.

"I'm one of them." He made a twisting motion with his mouth, and I had the feeling that he was making me wait. Then he said, "The other one is my father."

"Then it's probably him that I want to talk to."

"Could I ask what for?"

"My friend Tom said that Mr. Tull might have some work to be done."

"I'm not sure what kind there might be. Who did you say sent you?"

"Tom." For the life of me, I couldn't remember his last name at the moment.

"Oh, I know who you mean," he said. "Come on in here and wait for a few seconds."

He left me standing in the vestibule with my hat in my hand while he went through a sitting room and deeper into the house. A couple of minutes later, he came back and said his father would speak to me. Then he led me across the sitting room, through a dining room, and into an office or study. An older man sat at a large oak desk, looking at some papers by lamplight. The wall beyond him was one solid set of bookshelves, and the wall on my right had two tall cabinets, each with drawers halfway up and then a set of double doors. The man seemed to be lingering over whatever he was studying, for he made something of a flinch but kept his gaze on the papers.

"Here he is," said the son. Then to me he said, "This is my father, Lawrence Tull."

The old man turned in his chair and gave me a full look. Then he glanced at his son and said something that sounded like "Werewolf at eleven."

The young man said, "Of course," and left the room.

Tull the elder looked at me again and asked, "Was it Tom Devlin that sent you here?"

"Yes, it was, sir."

My eyes were adjusted now to the dim light of his den, and I had a full view of his pale bald head with its fringe of whitish hair. His face was pale as well, and he had plain blue eyes that looked worried but not shifty. His shirt was buttoned at the top and covered with a necktie, but his wrinkled neck was loose inside the collar. Between that and the drawn look to his face, he had the appearance of a man who had lost weight from an earlier period of his life. He was old enough to be my father and then some.

"And what did Tom tell you?"

"He told me you might have some work."

"I might. What kind of work did he say?"

"He said it might have to do with finding somebody."

"I see. What's your name, anyway, young man?"

"It's Jimmy Clevis, sir."

"Uh-huh. Have I heard of you?" His hands, which were in his lap, moved, and I saw that he held a leather cord with a tassel on the end and was pulling it through his closed left hand.

"I don't know. You may have. I was in a little scrape a while back."

"Yes, I might have." He looked at the tassel in his left palm. "Then tell me why you think you're the kind of person I might want to hire."

"Well, to begin with, when I set out to do a job, I stick with it. I don't push very easy." As I said it, I realized I owed it to Mr. Earlywine that I had the answer so quick at hand.

"What else?"

"I can get around all right without a lot of comforts. I can rough it or do without if I need to, to get the job done. I don't need to lay up in fine hotels and such."

He looked me over, as if I were a prizefighter or even a fighting dog he was getting ready to stake some money on. "I gather from what you've said that you know how to take care of yourself—not that I'm expecting any kind of danger."

"I've managed so far, when a couple of things have come my way."

He nodded, and then his eyes met mine. "Do you know how to keep things to yourself?"

"Oh, yeah."

"Then close the door and pull that chair over a little closer, and sit down."

Once I had the door closed, the old man seemed to soften. I had the feeling that it had something to do with his son.

He pulled at the loose skin on his throat, and then he spoke in a low tone. "Tom was right about my wanting to hire a man to find someone. To put it more specifically, I want to find someone from my past." He glanced at the closed door. "This has got to be confidential, you understand."

"A hundred percent."

His voice lowered even further than before. "I don't want you to mention any of this to my son Matthew. He helps manage my business affairs, but as far as I know, he doesn't have any knowledge about what I'm going to tell you. And I'd like to keep it that way until such time as I might choose to bring things to light."

I made a motion with my free hand. "Exactly as you say, Mr. Tull. I have no reason to do otherwise."

"Good." He fidgeted with the string and tassel for a couple of seconds and then looked straight at me. "I'm an old man," he said, "getting along in years. My wife is dead, and I'm pretty much alone. But I'm not washed up yet, and there's something I need to get done. I want to do it before much more time passes."

He paused, and I gave him the nod that I thought he was expecting.

"I want to tidy up an old loose end, you might say. Resolve something that I just let go and never tended to."

I gave him another nod, to help him along.

His nostrils opened as he took in a deep breath. "Years ago," he said, breathing out, "I had a love affair with a woman. A beautiful woman. She had a child, a little boy as I understood it, though I never saw him." He took another deliberate breath and moistened his lips before he went on. "I would like to find this son and meet him if that is possible."

"I can understand why."

"I have a little bit of information to go on, and I imagine you'll have to dig up a little more on your own. That was why I thought I might have to hire a detective." He seemed to hesitate before opening the next door. Then he said, "The woman's name was Dolores. She went on to marry a man named Bowden."

"And do you know what the boy was called?"

"I believe she named him Raymond."

"How old would he be now?"

"About your age. Twenty-eight."

"That's about as close as you can get. I'll be twenty-eight in a few months." I had a quick thought about Matthew, the son I'd met. I had placed him at a couple of years older than I was, which would be thirty or so. He might even be a year older than that. At any rate, the long-lost son would be younger than the legitimate son and heir. It all sized up pretty fast. Mr. Tull would have been married at the time of the affair, and the young woman

Dolores was not. None of this mattered much to me in the sense of whether I approved or not, as it was someone else's affair, and a long time gone. But I wondered how much it might matter to either son—or brother, as they might see it—if Mr. Tull decided to bring the old truth to light.

"I should have my doubts," he went on, "about sending a youngster out on business like this, that has taken up so much of my private thought for so many years. But you seem to have a level head on your shoulders, and you seem capable of going on a long trip by yourself."

"Going on my own doesn't bother me, and I can do my best with the work itself." I waited for a gesture of agreement and then said, "Where do you think this job will take me?"

"The woman lived in Paloma Springs, and the last I heard, she still lived there. Do you know where that is?"

"I've got it placed as south and west of here, before you go over the big mountains."

"That's right. It's just about due west of Pueblo, a couple of days' ride, and if you kept going on that road, you would go up and over the pass and on into Gunnison, and eventually you would come to Grand Junction. Just to give you an idea. You won't be going to any of those other places, of course. I would expect you to go southwest from here, as you said, go over the mountain, drop down into the ranch country, and follow that road until you come to Buena Vista, there on the Arkansas River. The trail follows that river for quite a ways and then holds south to Paloma Springs when the river turns toward the east."

"I haven't been there, but from what I've seen on maps and heard from others, that's the way I had it pictured."

"Good. Then it doesn't sound like too much of a journey for you?"

"Oh, not at all. And it'll give me a chance to see some new country."

"That's fine." He had his hands folded in his lap now. "I suppose we should talk about the pay."

I moved my head up and down. "Might as well."

"I've had it in mind to offer a hundred dollars at the outset, and then another hundred when you bring back a conclusive report."

That was twice what Mr. Earlywine offered, and it seemed less shady. "Sounds reasonable to me, Mr. Tull."

He did not move except for closing his eyelids and opening them. "I realize that this son, if you find him, may not want to meet me or have anything to do with this surprise of an unknown relation. I am prepared to accept that. But I expect you to make it known to him, and if he does not want to meet me, I expect at least a report of things, as I stated in my terms a moment ago."

"That seems like something I can do."

"And let me assure you there is nothing illegal or underhanded in what I'm asking you to do."

I assumed he was making a distinction between what he had done and what he was hiring me to do. "That's good," I said. "All I want to do is make an honest living—find decent work and do what I set out to do."

"I commend you for that. And I hope this trip goes off smoothly for you." He turned to his desk, opened an upper drawer on the right, and took out five twenty-dollar gold pieces. My spirits picked up right away, as I have always liked gold and silver coins better than whispering change. He rose from his chair and held the money toward me. As

I stood up, he said, "You have no idea how much pain and regret this whole thing has caused me over the years, and I hope I can resolve some of it."

I took the gold pieces without speaking, as I didn't have an answer for what he had just said.

We shook hands, and as he turned his blue eyes upon me, he said, "Please find my son for me if you can."

"I'll do my best."

He sat down and left me standing. "I have no doubt Matthew will show up as soon as you open the door."

"Very well," I said, not knowing what else to say. I turned and went out through the door, leaving behind me Mr. Lawrence Tull, to be alone with his secrets.

Matthew did not appear quite as soon as I expected, but I found him in the sitting room. He was not alone. Seated in a stuffed armchair at a right angle to his was a young and pretty blond woman.

Matthew rose from his seat as I came into the room. "I hope you had a satisfactory visit with my father."

"I did."

"I help as much as I can, but he is still very active in his affairs, and I know he has a great deal on his mind."

"That's normal, I guess."

"I'm sure it is." He turned to the young woman and said, "Let me introduce my fiancée, Miss Caroline Jackson."

As Miss Jackson rose from her chair, Matthew looked at me and said, "I don't believe I caught your name when you came in."

"I don't think I mentioned it, but it's Clevis. Jimmy Clevis."

"Yes. Well, Caroline, this is Mr. Clevis. I believe he's

here to agree to do some work for my father." Turning to me with a smile, he added, "Am I right?"

"We talked about it." I looked past the younger Tull and got a view of Miss Jackson. She was a shapely woman, with a pert bosom and a pretty neck. She had her hair pinned up in back, with a few wisps falling loose, and the stone on her hairpin matched the sky blue of her eyes. As she smiled at me, I sensed an air of confidence about her, as if she had the manners to treat young Mr. Tull with respect and admiration without having to be submissive.

"I'm pleased to meet you, Mr. Clevis. Are you from around here?"

"I've lived in the area for a couple of years, but I haven't gotten around town much. I've spent most of my time out in the ranch country."

"I see."

There was no telling whether these people had heard of me and the trouble I had been in or whether I was a complete stranger to them. Holding my hat in front of me with both hands, I made a slight bowing motion and said, "It's a pleasure to meet you." Then I turned to Matthew and held out my hand. "Likewise with you."

He shook my hand and gave me a look of great assurance—so great that I thought he would like to open me up like a melon and find out what it was I had been discussing with his father. But he said nothing and just led me to the door.

On the way, I caught a glimpse of a painting on the wall. It showed a girl on a balcony, with flowers on each side, behind an iron railing. I had the quick impression that the painting had been selected because of the girl's resemblance to Miss Jackson, but then I thought no more of it as Matthew Tull opened the door and ushered me out with a slow nod.

I heard the door close as I walked down the steps toward the tall horse waiting for me. Although I had the stone foundation and green shutters in the corner of my sight, I did not look at the house until I was up and into the saddle. Then, as I turned the horse around, I caught a glimpse of the two dormer windows, each with its little eave casting a shadow like an eyebrow.

Chapter Three

Back on the main street of town, I thought I should go see Mr. Earlywine before long and tell him I had other work and couldn't accept his offer. But the idea of going to see him wasn't very attractive, and I thought I might put him off for a while. For one thing, I had the feeling that he would still try to convince me and would want to quiz me on the job I accepted. For another thing, the only people I'd talked to for more than a minute in the last day or so had been older men, and I thought I'd like a change in scenery before I went and faced Mr. Earlywine.

I followed the main street south to the river, thumped across the plank bridge, and rode into Mexican town. Up ahead on my right would be Chanate's butcher shop, not yet within my view. I could picture my friend standing at the butcher block, slicing a flitch of bacon, with chains of sausage hanging all around. I could almost smell the *chorizo*. Maybe a little later I would drop in on Chanate to tell him where I was going. I could also take leave of his wife, Tina, who always treated me well and served good meals beneath the painting of the Last Supper.

It gave me a happy feeling to be in Mexican town, as if in crossing the river I had left my worries and troubles behind. I suppose on both sides of any river, if a fellow went far enough, he could find old men who were worried about protecting their secrets, but things like that didn't touch me in the places I went to on this side. I had good friends here, people who took me into their houses and treated me like one of their own. They didn't ask what they called indiscreet questions, and although they knew I had had some trouble, they knew that none of it had anything to do with them. Maybe they passed a doubtful word or two behind my back, and I wouldn't blame them, but the door was always open and they always said they were happy to see Yeemee.

First among my friends here was Chanate, named for the blackbird, and his wife, Clementina. They were the ones I went to when I needed to be bolstered by the feelings of friendship and home. On the same level of confidence, but with another ripple as well, was their niece Magdalena, or Nena. Now that I knew I was going away for a while, I set aside the indecision I had had the day before, and I decided to visit her first today. It was late enough in the morning that she should be up and about.

I turned left and rode down the dirt street for three blocks until I came to her house, a small stuccoed building on a plain lot. I swung down from the tall horse, tied him to the hitching rail, and knocked on the front door. In less than a moment, the door opened.

"Yimi," she said. "What a surprise." Actually, in Spanish they say "What a miracle," but it means surprise. Our conversation, as usual, ran in Spanish.

"Good morning, Nena. I came by to say hello."

"How nice. Please come in." She stood aside to let me pass.

I took off my hat as I went in, and then I turned to look at her. Her long, dark hair, which she sometimes kept tied back, hung loose over her shoulders. She had put on red lipstick the same color as her solid round earrings, and the red made a lovely contrast with her tan complexion. She was wearing a plain, bronze-colored cotton dress, which set off her figure in a way that brought up sparks in me like always. No wonder I had been afraid to see her the day before, and no wonder I wanted to kick myself in the ass for it now.

With her right hand she combed her hair back over her shoulder. "Tell me, Yimi, what can I offer you? A coffee? Something to eat?"

"A coffee would be just fine."

"Let me see." She stepped into the kitchen area, opened the door on the woodstove, and poked inside with an iron rod. I could see coals glowing as she stepped aside to pick a few sticks out of the woodbox. She chunked the firewood into the stove and closed the door, then turned to me and smiled. "I have some tamales I can heat, also."

"That seems fine to me." I stood and watched as she put a pan of water on the stove top and then slid a *comal,* or flat griddle, next to it.

She straightened up and smiled again, her green eyes flashing. "And what news do you have, Yimi?"

"Not much. It seems that I have a job."

"Oh, that's good. It's good to have work."

"That's true."

A serious expression crossed her face. "Are you going back to work on a ranch?"

I figured she meant the wide loop. "No, this is a different kind of work. I think it's all right. Tome recommended it to me."

"Oh, yes. Tome is very wise. He knows many things."

"He does."

"And so this job is—what kind?"

"A man, an older man, over here in town, wants me to go find a son for him. A son who has been lost to him. He wants to know the son before much time passes."

"I hope you can help him, then. An old man should be able to see his sons again at the end of his life."

"He has a son living with him, but this other one he has never seen. I think it is something that has given him shame."

Magdalena raised and lowered her eyebrows. "How sad. A dark spot in the rice. And now he is repenting, and he wants to amend things."

"That's the way it seems."

"I hope you can find the son for him so that he can be at peace. Do you go very far?"

"I have to go to a place called Paloma Springs, which is at least three days of travel from here."

"Oh. In what direction?"

"South and west."

"Not so far as Durango?"

I thought she might have associated the name I mentioned with a place down that way named Pagosa Springs. "Oh, no," I said. "Half that distance, or less."

"That's good. Do you go alone?"

"Yes, I do."

"Well, I hope you have a good trip, without any trouble, and that you see many nice things."

"Thank you. I hope so, too."

She held her open hand over the stove top to test the heat, then did the same above the *comal.* Next she turned to the sideboard, where she took a metal lid off the top of a clay pot.

"These are good tamales. My aunt made them."

"Oh, then I'm sure they're good."

"You'll see." She lifted out four moist-looking tamales and set them on the *comal.* Only the faintest sizzling sound came from the contact, so I imagined it would be a few minutes until things heated up right.

"And Tome," she said, "he is fine?"

"Oh, yes. Just fine."

"And when does he come here again?"

"I suppose when there's another dance."

She laughed. "He is very good, Tome is."

All the Mexicans liked Tome because he spoke Spanish, though sometimes with the edges knocked off, and because he knew his manners around them. They respected him because of his age, and his glasses, and the many things that he knew. And they indulged him. They all knew he wanted to find a good woman who could cook well, either an old maid or a widow. So they smiled when he came to their dances and paid attention to the *solteronas* and the *viudas.*

"He is a good friend," I said. "He calls himself my uncle."

She laughed again. "How gracious."

"So," I said after a few seconds of silence, "what news do you have?"

She brushed back a few loose hairs from the side of her forehead. "It's possible that I might be going on a trip, also."

"Really?"

"Yes. You remember my cousin, Rosa Linda."

"Of course." A picture came to mind of a clean, innocent-looking girl in a yellow dress. Not long after I had met Rosa Linda the first couple of times, Magdalena asked me if I was interested in her. I didn't know whether Magdalena meant that being interested in her cousin would be all right or whether she was asking out of a personal interest of her own, so I felt as if I was sitting on the fence.

"Well, we are waiting to hear from her family, about the health of my grandmother."

"It would be Rosa Linda's grandmother as well?"

"Yes, of course."

"And they live in Colorado Springs?"

"Yes. You remember." She turned to the stove, tapped one of the tamales, and turned back to face me. "Anyway, my grandmother is not very well, and I may have to go to Colorado Esprín."

"I understand. And I hope your grandmother gets better."

"Thank you."

"And Rosa Linda? I hope she's fine."

"Oh, yes. She is at Rancho Alegre right now, visiting with others in the family."

"Rancho Alegre? Where's that? Near Colorado Espreen?"

"Farther. It is to the south and west of Pueblo."

"Then she is quite a ways from home."

"For the present. But I hope to see her if I go to Esprín. She will come back early if my grandmother is not better."

A small popping sound came from the *comal,* and Nena turned to scoot the tamales around and keep them from sticking. The smell of corn husk, grease, and cornmeal rose on the warm air.

Nena spoke again. "Do you think you will pass through Colorado Esprín on your trip?"

"I suppose I could." I pictured the map in my mind. "When I finish my work in Paloma Springs, I could take the road towards Pueblo and then, before I got there, turn north to Espreen."

"I would be happy to have you visit at our family's house, if I were to be there."

"I would enjoy that. How would I know if you were there?"

"I could send you a letter to one of the towns you pass through."

"That would be fine. Two towns I would go through would be Cañon City and Florence. I can check for mail in both places, in case you want to send me a message to tell me where you will be."

"What is the name of the second town?"

"Florence. It's close to Cañon City."

"Very well." She turned the tamales over on the *comal,* and the smell of the scorched corn husk was promising.

"Did your aunt make a great many tamales?"

"Yes, she did. And they are very good. Actually, I helped her. It is too much for one person. Another *señora* helped also."

"That's good."

Nena laughed. "The other *señora* told a joke. I just remembered it."

"Can you tell it to me?"

"Oh, yes. It goes like this. There was a man, very sick, and he knew he was going to die. He was lying in bed, thinking of how little time he had left, when he smelled tamales. Oh, how wonderful. He knew his dear wife was making him some tamales before he would leave this world, and hers were the best, the very best.

"The rich smell lifted his spirits, and he found the strength to get out of bed, take up his cane, and with slow, painful steps make his way to the kitchen. There was his dear wife, with a large steamer pot on the stove and a big bowl of dough on the table. She was using a wooden spoon to spread the dough onto the corn leaf, and at the edge of the table was a plate with the first tamales she had taken out of the steamer.

"The sick husband came close to the table, with one hand on his cane, and reached for a tamale with his other hand. Then, *pum!* She hit him on the back of the hand with the big wooden spoon.

" 'Leave them alone, you fool!' said the wife. 'Those tamales are for the funeral!' "

We were both laughing then, standing in Magdalena's warm kitchen. Her young, pretty face and her bright red earrings made death seem like something a long ways away. I sure found her company lifting my own spirits, and I thought it would be well worth my time to make a detour to Colorado Springs.

My visit with Chanate was a short one, as he was taking a detailed order from a woman whose daughter was getting married. There would be a supper and a dance. Not only did the woman want twenty-two kilos of pork meat for *carnitas* and enough lard to cook it all in, but she also needed eight kilos of tripe to make the *menudo* for the morning after the dance. Chanate said he thought he would have to kill two cows to get enough tripe, and he asked the woman if she might like beef instead of pork for the main meat. She said no, but if he was going to kill two cows she would like to have the tongues set aside for her. After that, they started back through the whole order, including how small he should cut up the pork meat. When she asked to try a bit of sausage and then asked him if he would give her a discount if she bought beef instead of pork, I could see I was in for a long wait. So I took leave of Chanate, gave my regards to Tina, and said I would be back in about a week, with the favor of God. Of the things I have learned from the Mexicans, one is not to say, with any sense of certainty, that he will be back on thus-and-such a day. One cannot predict the future, and it is wrong to think that he can. So with that provision, I went on my way.

The sun was not yet straight overhead then, when I rode across the bridge and dropped back into the white part of town. I felt pretty good. I had money in my pocket, warm food in my stomach, and a paying job to carry out. I wouldn't have minded staying longer at Magdalena's, but I didn't have any claim on her time, and if I didn't dawdle around, I could get half a day's travel behind me yet today. All I had to do was drop in on Mr. Earlywine, buy a few provisions, and roll up my camp.

I found Mr. Earlywine's house just as I had done the day before. It didn't look as sunbaked as it had seemed when the sun came in from the west, but it still had a lone and lifeless appearance. My horse's hooves made thudding sounds until I stopped him and bailed off. Then everything was quiet. With the reins in my hand, I went to the front door and rapped on the panel. I rapped a second time, and then a third without raising an answer.

I led my horse around the edge of the house, calling out to ask if there was anybody home. The back yard came into view, unchanged, with the empty chicken house and the shed with weeds all around it. No shade had crept out from the house yet, and no chairs sat in the lee of the building. The only thing worth noting was that the back door was half open.

Even as I walked up to the open door, I had an uneasy feeling that I was going to find something out of order. I called out again and, still getting no answer, I came close enough to peek in.

I saw a man's foot—or rather, a man's shoe pointing upward from the floor. Whoever was wearing that shoe had a thick ankle covered with a gray wool sock, and he wore common drab pants just like the ones Mr. Earlywine had been wearing the day before. Then I saw the other foot and leg, and I was pretty sure it was Mr. Earlywine lying on the floor.

At that point I could have told myself that this was none of my business, but I didn't have that presence of mind. Nor could I recall Tome's sage advice about going in through back doors. Instead, I dropped the reins on the ground and stepped into the house.

It was Mr. Earlywine, all right, lying flat on his back with his belly sticking up. His dull eyes and dark mouth were open, and I could tell he wasn't going to move again under his own power. He hadn't shaved since I had seen him last, and a fly was crawling across the stubble on his cheek toward the corner of his mouth. It looked as if there was a larger fly on his forehead, and then I saw that it was a bullet hole.

I had a sinking feeling. With Mr. Earlywine past all

help, all I could think of was myself, and plenty came to me all at once. Here I was, with a dead man on my hands—and not a man who had died from swallowing a chicken bone or sliding off a barn roof, as men of Mr. Earlywine's girth sometimes did. He had been killed in cold blood, I had probably been one of the last people to talk to him, and we had talked about things, if only vaguely, that were no doubt related to the dark spot on his forehead. I was going to have to report this and answer a long chain of questions. If I didn't, but just left town and let someone else find the body, I could have some real trouble at my back. After all, I had been here twice in full daylight, and for as much as the house sat off by itself, someone would have seen me come or go. To protect the good name of Jimmy Clevis and to keep from having the law sent after me, I was going to have to tell about talking business with a blackmailer and then finding him dead. Good old Jimmy Clevis, talking to the law about another dead man that crossed his path.

And talk I did. I spent a long afternoon in the sheriff's office, telling about how I came to meet Mr. Earlywine, what he told me and proposed to me, why I declined his offer, and what I had done with every minute of my time since I had left him smoking his cigar in the shade of his house. I was pressed for details about a lean stranger I hadn't noticed in any detail, I was quizzed on who the greasers might be, and I was asked a hundred times if I was sure the deceased had never mentioned a name. I felt as if I had been pumped empty by the time the sheriff let me go. He told me that if I didn't hear from him by morning I was free to leave on my trip.

Out on the street, I had to muster up all of my self-control to keep from going to the Jack-Deuce. I wanted a drink. But I also knew I didn't need to be answering any more questions, or hearing gossip, or addling my brain with the demon.

Furthermore, I was worried about protecting what little reputation I had. I was sure Mr. Tull would hear about my being caught up in this mess, as the sheriff would be checking on my whereabouts, and I imagined Mr. Tull would wonder why I was poking around in things that had nothing to do with the job he had hired me for. I wished things were so simple that I could go up to him and say, "You see, I just had to tell the man I would rather work for you, but when I got there he was dead." But things were not that simple.

Once a fellow is in the middle of something like this, he can look back and see where he might have done things differently. For me, it was the moment when Mr. Earlywine told me I could think about it. I knew then that I didn't want to take the job, and I should have turned it down at that time. But I didn't, and here I was. It was a small comfort to recognize to myself that I had been right about the possibility of trouble. If I was that smart, I should have done more about it, and I wouldn't have gotten in this far.

I doubted that the sheriff would want to keep me around, though, so I went back to my camp and sorted through my few belongings. I didn't have a packhorse, so I was going to have to travel light. I had finished making the rope halter, and I imagined it might come in handy at some point, so I stuffed it in my warbag. I checked to see that my sheath knife had a good edge on it, and I gave my rifle and scabbard a checking-over. Beyond those things and a few articles of clothing, I didn't have anything I couldn't leave behind. I had been boiling my coffee in a tin can and roasting my dinner meat on a sharpened willow stick, so I didn't have any kitchenware to worry about. I would have to buy my food a little at a time, and as soon as I bought a can of peaches or tomatoes, I would be back in business with something to boil water in. I figured I could buy my first bait of grub on my way out of town in the morning.

As the evening wore on, I began to feel less of the weight of any knowledge I had of Mr. Earlywine. I was sorry for him, in a small way, as I thought of him laid out on the floor of his dusty house with no one to care much about him. But I didn't have anything to do with his death, and I didn't have to let someone make me feel as if I did. There was trouble here, but it wasn't mine. Thieving and blackmailing, and the things that people did to be blackmailed—embezzlement, fornication, murder, or acts even more hideous to mention—were likely to show up wherever very many people came together. And even though the current mess was not mine, it would be good for me to be taking a trip somewhere else, in a different direction from Mr. Earlywine and his problems.

Chapter Four

The trip to Paloma Springs went well enough. On the first day out I got into tall mountains, but I was riding a horse to match. He climbed right along. In the afternoon a rainstorm built up, so I spent about an hour underneath a big pine tree, standing near the trunk on a carpet of dry pinecones while my horse stood with his head lowered. I had my slicker draped across the saddle to keep my clothes, bedding, rifle, and food from getting wet. A rainstorm has a way of closing off the rest of the world, and I enjoyed being so far from everything except my immediate surroundings. From where I stood I could see a ridge of three mountains, all forested, reaching toward the clouds. The timber, dense and green, stood up straight on the mountainsides and took in the silver rain that fell in sheets. I was happy for the forest drinking in the fresh moisture, and I didn't mind the water dripping off the brim of my hat.

The next day I crossed the pass at about ten thousand feet, with the tall horse wheezing a little. In the afternoon I rode through Fairplay, a small town in ranch country. There I saw a woman standing in a doorway. She was a blond-haired woman with a good shape, maybe five or ten years older than I was. She stood with her hand on her hip and gave me a lingering gaze as I rode past.

On the third day, I reached the Arkansas River near Buena Vista. It rained again, but not so heavy as on the first day, and I was able to find dry firewood along the river. The fourth day broke clear and dry, and I rode into Paloma Springs on a warm afternoon.

As a general rule, food held a higher place on my list than it had done for the past few days. I had been willing to live on jerky and biscuits and water, and coffee once a day boiled in a can, because I felt I owed it to Mr. Tull. I had told him I didn't need to be coddled, and on top of that I felt as if I had to redeem myself with the world at large for having had anything to do with Mr. Earlywine. After four days of short rations, though, and no drink, and no contact with women except for the glance I returned in Fairplay, I thought I had been virtuous long enough. When I rode into Paloma Springs, I kept a weather eye out for a place that served meals.

The restaurant was called El Cuervo Azul, and on the white stuccoed wall outside, below the name of the place, there was a painting of a bluish bird in a cage. Inside the establishment, the real *cuervo azul,* a blue-black crow, perched in a large wicker cage. An older lady about fifty years old, dressed in gray and black, waited on me. When she learned that I spoke Spanish, she became quite talkative.

She had some very good chicken soup today. She was having trouble with the coyotes, and one of them had run off with a hen in his mouth, in broad daylight. She shut up the chickens at night in the *gallinero,* but she had to let them out in the daytime. And then a coyote so bold, he comes like that. Nevertheless, she had very good chickens and very good soup.

The mention of chicken soup reminded me of a time, once at a *rancho,* when I had a bowl of such soup in front of me. The meat was all boiled and falling apart, so that the tendons hung loose on a drumstick—or so it seemed as I picked at a piece of leg. I had the large end of it in my mouth when I realized it was a chicken's foot, boiled soft. I took it out of my mouth, but I couldn't undo what I had done so far. I had ingested some parts of that scaly chicken leg, and the germs or bugs or whatever I might call them were in me. It wasn't quite like the stories of greenhorns who thought they were eating chicken and found out it was snake, or who praised the stew and learned that the squaws had chewed the meat to make it tender—but it nearly gagged me all the same, and it made me wary of chicken soup.

The *señora* said she also had some very good lamb. It was so well-liked that a fresh lamb did not last but a few days, which was better than in the other places where even the beans stayed in the pot for a week. Not here. She had so many clients who loved her cooking that she had to boil a new pot of beans every day. And the lamb, it was killed on Friday, and today was barely Tuesday. It was delicious, cut into chunks and cooked in red chile, and very clean. Not like in those other places, where they served you meat and said it was beef, and then you got a stomachache and it was probably meat from a burro.

I could feel pangs of fear going through my own stomach, but I went ahead and ordered a plate of lamb and beans. The meal appeared in a few minutes, and it was every bit as good as she said it was. I asked her if she had beer, and she said no but she could get some. I heard her go back to the kitchen and call into another room, which I imagined to be the living quarters. Within five minutes, she brought me a mug of beer that was not very cold but welcome all the same.

She asked me what a young man like myself was doing here, and I told her I was on an errand for another man. Oh, that was very good. I told her that I was looking for a Mrs. Bowden, who had a son named Raymond. She shook her head and said that she didn't know many of the Americans. Then she added that she was sure they were good people, and many of them had nice houses on the west side of town.

I drank a second mug of beer and mopped up the last of my meal with a flour tortilla. Then I paid the *señora* and walked out into the sunny afternoon. I was feeling slow and lazy, but I had work to do, so I led my horse over to a low hummock of sand and stepped into the stirrup from there.

On the west side of the little town, I saw an older man sitting on a chair in the shade of a house. He was painting another chair, putting a dark brown trim around the glossy white. He was a Mexican man, so I asked him in Spanish if he knew of a Señora Bowden. Then I thought to mention her first name.

"O, sí, Dolores," he said. *"Doña Dolores."*

I told him I was looking for her house, and he pointed a block away to a street that ran uphill with shade trees on each side. Hers was the third one on the right, he said, the one with the railing.

I asked if he thought she was at home, and his face took

on a quiet expression. Oh, no, he said. She was not alive anymore, and the house was all alone. That was the word he used. In English, people would just say empty.

I thanked him and rode past a house with a back yard full of goats, past another house where the smell of corn tortillas came wafting out, then past the corner house, where a large-boned white woman stood in the front yard and flailed dust out of a rug as two little towheaded children looked on. I turned at the corner and rode up the hill to the third house.

It was a larger dwelling than the ones below, and it looked as if it might have been comfortable at one time, with a broad patio and elm trees on the side and an outdoor fireplace in back. Now the house was all closed up, with iron grates on the windows and doors, a six-foot fence made of iron rails, and a chain and padlock on the gate. The windows on the street side were boarded up as well, and cobwebs hung on the ironwork enclosing the front door. It gave me a sad feeling to have come all this way and to see a dry, empty husk of life where the woman Dolores had lived.

I dismounted and walked up to the rail fence. I saw parched rosebushes clinging to a trellis and a thirsty-looking lilac bush by the back door. Closer to me, on this side of the door, I saw a large clay *olla* standing on the paving stones of the patio. It was covered with dust, and it looked empty. I imagined it had dead bugs and scraps of windblown weeds inside, and I would have taken a look if it hadn't been out of reach.

I stood gazing for a long moment or two, wondering what my next step was going to be, when I saw a man standing in front of the house up the hill on my left. He was a pale man, looking even more so with the sunlight glaring through what little hair he had on top. He was wearing a long-sleeved white shirt and pressed pants, as if he had just come home from a store or office.

I led my horse over to the corner of his yard, where a low rock wall separated the properties in front of the iron railing. "How do you do?" I began. "My name's Jimmy Clevis, and I was hoping to find out a little about the people who used to live next door here."

"Oh, the Bowdens," he said with a solemn look. "Very nice people. They've both gone on, though."

I decided to make it seem as if my interest was in both Mr. and Mrs. Bowden, as that seemed more respectable. Along the way, I hoped, I would pick up what I needed to know about Raymond. "I'm sorry to hear that," I said. "Did you know them well?"

"We lived next door to each other for more than fifteen years," said the man, lifting his eyebrows in a glance toward the abandoned yard. "Mr. Bowden wasn't very talkative, but my wife knew his wife somewhat."

"Oh, I see."

He gave me a close look. "How do you come to be interested in them?"

"Oh, an old friend of Mrs. Bowden's knew that I was passing through this way and asked me to look them up."

"Uh-huh. Let me see if my wife is free to talk," he said. "We can sit on the front porch."

I tied my horse to the railing and waited on my side of the stone wall until the man went into the house and came out again through the front door. A woman appeared behind him, carrying a tray with three glasses. He called me over, so I went around to the walkway and made my way to the porch. Meanwhile, the woman went into the house and came out with a pitcher of what looked like lemonade.

"By the way," said the man, "my name is Eugene Allard. This is my wife."

Mrs. Allard smiled, as if she was used to not having a first name, and poured three glasses of pale liquid. I took off my hat and had a seat just as she handed me my glass.

The lemonade was sweet as syrup and not very cold, so I took only a small sip. Mr. and Mrs. Allard, though, drained a glass each.

"That hits the spot," he said as his wife refilled their glasses.

She sat down and looked at me. She had a soft, chubby face and kind, brown eyes. "Eugene tells me you're interested in the Bowdens."

"Yes, I am. I was surprised not to find either of them alive. I should say sorry, actually."

"Oh, Mr. Bowden's been gone for a good six years now, and Dolores has been gone for almost two."

"I see." I motioned with my head in the direction of the vacant house. "I don't have much of an idea of Mr. Bowden at all. What kind of a man was he, anyway?"

Neither of them said anything for several seconds, nor did they look at each other. Then Mrs. Allard said, "He was a serious man." She turned to her husband and asked, "Wouldn't you say so?"

Mr. Allard pushed out his lip and nodded. "There was no monkey business with him. He left early to go to his store, and when he wasn't there, he stayed close to home."

"He enjoyed himself in little ways, though," said Mrs. Allard. "He would sit in the yard when the weather was nice, and he would smoke his pipe. For several years he had a bulldog named Buller that would sit at his feet."

"Did he die rather suddenly?"

"No," answered Mrs. Allard. "He grew thin over a period of a couple of years and didn't spend very much time outside, and then he passed on."

"That must have been difficult for his wife. What kind of a person was she?"

"She was more cheerful," said Mrs. Allard, "but you could tell that life wasn't always happy for her."

"Oh?"

"Well, between a husband who was that serious and a son who wasn't that easy to deal with . . ." Mrs. Allard hesitated.

"That's right," I said. "I understand she had a son. But tell me more about her. The name was Dolores, wasn't it? One of the men down below called her *Doña Dolores*."

"Yes. That was what the Mexicans called her."

"Of course, she was Mexican, too," put in Mr. Allard.

I remembered Mr. Tull saying she was beautiful.

"Yes," said his wife, "but she was very nice, and I think she must have come from a decent family. You could tell it from the things she did. She played the piano and baked bread that always smelled so lovely. In the summer she brought out the geraniums in clay pots, and she usually had a songbird or two that she would hang outside in a cage."

"It seems as if they might have been an unlikely couple," I said.

"Oh, I don't know," she answered. "They got along. He was a little older, and they both had something of an earlier life."

"Here in Paloma Springs?"

She seemed to hesitate for a moment and then spoke. "No, in other places. I don't know where-all he had been before he met her, but he had some older children that were on their own. I know she used to live in Cañon City. That's where she met him, and when he bought the hardware store in town, they came here together."

"They were *married* in Cañon City," said Mr. Allard.

"I didn't mean to suggest they weren't," said his wife. "She was very nice. And very clean. She swept all the time, inside and out."

"Did she always live in Cañon City before she came here?"

"I don't think so," answered Mrs. Allard. "I believe she lived in Pueblo. Raymond was probably born there. You know he wasn't Mr. Bowden's."

"I knew that. Or at least I'd been given to understand it."

Mrs. Allard looked in the direction of the abandoned house. "She didn't talk much about that part of her life before she met Mr. Bowden. I think she had had some trouble then."

Mr. Allard spoke up. "He was a jealous sort, too. And he never got along very well with Raymond. Not that I could blame him." He took a drink from his glass.

"Oh, was Raymond troublesome?" I asked.

"Not when he was a boy," said Mrs. Allard. "He did normal things—like he had a pet raccoon for a while. That was before Mr. Bowden got Buller. Then Raymond had a boneshaker, which he spilled at least once a day at the bottom of the hill. But when he got older, about fifteen or sixteen, he turned rebellious."

"They never whipped him," said her husband. "He

sassed both of them, and he wouldn't work in the store. But he always cadged money out of his mother so he could buy cigarettes at the drugstore. And I know for a fact that he bought whiskey, too. He had something in his blood."

"A little wild, then?" I suggested.

Mrs. Allard answered right away. "He was a handsome young man, and not without manners when he wanted, but he wasn't happy at home. I might say he wasn't satisfied with what he had."

I looked down at my glass and then up at her. "That's too bad. Does he still live around here?"

"No. He left home several years ago. When Mrs. Bowden passed away, he came back to settle the affairs, and then he closed up the house and went back to Pueblo."

"Oh, does he live in Pueblo now, then?"

"Yes, as far as I know. He had a good friend in that town, and I believe he associates with him there."

"Do you happen to know the friend's name?"

Mrs. Allard looked at her husband, who said, "Jeffrey. That's his last name."

I nodded and then turned to Mrs. Allard. "You say he was handsome. I understand his mother was, also."

"Oh, she was a pretty lady, especially when she was younger. Mr. Bowden couldn't have done better."

I cast my line. "Raymond must have liked the girls."

She gave me a look as if she was surprised by my comment. "I'm sure he did. But I think the nice ones were warned to stay away from him."

"Not without reason, it sounds like." I looked at Mr. Allard. "Like you say, he must have had something in his blood."

He frowned. "Some of it could have been taken out of

him, if they had been willing to whip him. There were times when I felt like offering."

I moved my head up and down, trying to show regret about no one whipping the lad.

"He was a nice boy when he was young," said the wife, "and you would have thought the presence of a man would have had better effect. But he turned out to be difficult."

"And now he lives in Pueblo, you say."

"Yes," she answered. "You know how sometimes the young people like to go to a larger town."

"That they do." I turned to Mr. Allard, as if he could best answer my next question. "Do you know if he has a particular line of work?"

"I wouldn't expect it." He took a sip of lemonade and gave me a crosswise glance. "Are you planning to look him up?"

"I think I should try."

"On behalf of a friend of Mrs. Bowden's, I think you said."

"Yes." I looked at my lemonade and could not bring myself to take a drink of it.

He looked close at me. "What kind of a friend?"

I thought for a couple of seconds. These people had been forthcoming with me, and I didn't think I would queer the deal on any further information by answering straight, so I did. "I'm looking for information on behalf of Raymond's natural father."

Mr. Allard's jaw tightened. "I'd say it's rather late in the day for that, for a father to want to recognize a son, when the woman wasn't good enough for him before. So what if she was a Mexican? Mr. Bowden found her good enough, even if he had to put up with her son."

"I don't know anything about those earlier years, except that there was a child born. If I knew more, such as what you've told me, and which I appreciate, I might not have come this far. But I signed on to help an old man try to find a long-lost son before he died."

"I suppose he has a right to try, regardless of how the son was born," said Mr. Allard. "But I think he'd do just as well to leave it alone. And if you find Raymond, I think you'll find him to be a sulky, ungrateful sort."

"From what you've mentioned, I wouldn't be surprised." I turned to Mrs. Allard. "By the way, do you know what Mrs. Bowden's maiden name was?"

She seemed to have tightened up, also. "Yes, I do. I would think the man who hired you to ask questions would have told you. What's his name?"

"Tull," I said, feeling I'd been made to confess. "Lawrence Tull."

She shook her head. "I never heard Mrs. Bowden mention that name, not either part of it." Then, as if she was keeping up her part of a bargain, she said, "Her maiden name was Correa. Dolores Correa. That's who she was when she met your Mr. Tull, and I can't say he did her any good."

"I don't have any reason to disagree with you, ma'am."

She softened again. "I'm sorry. I don't mean to suggest that it's any of your fault."

"Thank you," I answered. "And like I told your husband, I took on a job to try to find someone, and I didn't give much thought to what else I might learn along the way. But I've started, and I need to try to do what I set out to do."

The husband spoke up. "Go ahead. It's not your fault. But I think he'd been better off to leave it all alone."

"I can't judge that," I said. "I've never had any children."

"Neither have I," he answered. "But I've seen a few others, and I've had some idea of where they came from."

The afternoon shadows were starting to reach out when I left Paloma Springs. I had plenty to think on. Mr. Tull hadn't told me as much as he might have, but there were certainly some things he didn't know, either—most important among them, that Dolores wasn't alive. He must have been able to keep track of her long enough to know where she ended up, here in Paloma Springs with Mr. Bowden, but his source must have dropped out of touch, maybe even died. There was no telling.

My thoughts kept returning to Dolores. I had the most sympathy for her out of all these people, dead and alive. She seemed to have made a tolerable life for herself, in spite of having had an affair with a man who let her go and having been married to a man whose idea of pleasure was smoking his pipe with his bulldog. And then having a son like Raymond. I could imagine her in the railed-in patio, setting out her flowers and her songbird.

I had to keep reminding myself not to judge Mr. Tull. That wasn't my job. But as I gave him more thought, I formed a better idea of what the story really was. Something I had gathered earlier seemed to be confirmed now—that his affair with Dolores Correa had been adulterous on his part. Now it seemed as if he had been willing to have a Mexican woman for his mistress but no more. With his wife now dead, he would go so far as to recognize his son. He might have been afraid to go any further. It was hard for me to guess how much of his pain and regret, as he had called it, was based on guilt and how much was based on shame. I didn't know. Secrets worked in strange ways. But if any of his secret was based on a sense that the woman was beneath him, as Mr. Allard had suggested, I couldn't admire him very much. I could still sympathize with him and try to do my job, but I couldn't help feeling that some part of him was empty.

I looked over my shoulder at the town in its shadows. *Good-bye, Doña Dolores,* I thought. *Que en paz descanses*. May you rest in peace.

Then I clucked to the tall horse and held on to my reins as he stretched his head forward. An image came back to me of Mr. Earlywine, a heavyset man lying on his back with his mouth open and a dark spot on his forehead. I suppose I thought of him because I realized I was headed for Pueblo after all.

Chapter Five

I rode into Cañon City two days later, as the shadows of afternoon were stretching into evening. That leg of my trip had been a solitary one, dry and dusty except when the horse and I dropped into the river bottom. I had long hours to myself, plenty of time to think about Mr. Tull, his son Matthew, Doña Dolores, Raymond Bowden, and even, from time to time, the unfortunate Mr. Earlywine. I also gave thought to myself and how virtuous I was being, back on slim rations and not indulging myself. Of course, I didn't have any other choice, out on a lone trail and a long ways between towns, but I still took the opportunity to compliment myself on being dutiful.

When I got to Cañon City, which was a little over halfway between Paloma Springs and Pueblo, I thought I might relax a little for one evening. I also told myself that while I was out and about, I might run into someone who knew something about Dolores in years past. I found a livery stable for the horse, and with another four bits I got a bed of fresh straw where I could leave my belongings and come back to sleep after I had gotten something to eat and drink.

Not far from the livery, toward the east edge of town, I found a roadhouse named Johns Castle. Like several other buildings I had seen, including a couple of stately mansions, this place was made out of sandstone. Inside, I saw a painted portrait of one Elwood Johns, the original proprietor. Two other patrons pointed out his picture to me. They seemed to enjoy being experts on local history, for the benefit of travelers, and they lost little time in telling me that the sandstone came from nearby and had been quarried by convict labor. Some of the early building, they said, had been done in the day of a man named Anson Rudd, a founder of the city and a leader in civic affairs. He had also been a poet and a lively character in the community.

They spoke of others as well—I remember a Robison and a Penrose—who had made big money in mining, railroads, and ranching, but the mention of someone named Rudd gave me a momentary twinge. I had had a little trouble not too much earlier, up north by Monetta, with a fellow named Axel Rudd. But that fellow was a sour, sarcastic type, far from being a poet or civic leader. I assumed that the similar names were just a coincidence, but I still found myself looking over my shoulder now and then, to see if some phantom relative might have a surprise for me.

The beer was cold, and as I settled into enjoying my second glass of it, one of my two new friends announced that he had to leave. That left me and the other fellow standing at the bar, with him on my right. He was red-haired, taller than average, and loose-bodied. From a side view I saw that he had a recessed chin, so that the jaw part of his head seemed to go straight down from his lower gum and then the skin and flesh sloped on a diagonal down to the throat.

"My name's Kelly Kelly," he said, holding out his hand to shake. "My mother stuttered. When she named me."

I gave a light laugh, as I thought I was supposed to. "My name's Jimmy Clevis," I said. Damned if I was going to say anything about my mother in a place like this, and I was beginning to have my doubts about mentioning Doña Dolores.

"Where you from?" he asked.

"Up north."

"Just like back east and down south, only different. What line of work are you in, up north?"

I didn't know if he was making fun of me, but I answered him straight so I could ask questions of him. "I was doing ranch work. Then a fellow hired me to run a personal errand for him. How about yourself?"

"I did blacksmithing and iron work, but then I hurt my back. If it gets better, I'll be back at the forge with the hammer and tongs. If not, I might take to clerkin'."

It was hard to imagine what kind of clerk he might make, and he gave the impression that if he did clerk somewhere, the proprietor would do well to watch the cash box.

"Bein' in between work, though," he said, "I've been forced to sell some things that have been in the family a long while. Hate to do it, but a man's got to get by."

"Isn't that the truth?"

"Tell me what you think of it," he said, and he swung a

gold watch on a chain in the air next to me. Then he laid it in his palm.

I saw the initials *P.R.* engraved on the plating.

"It belonged to my grandfather," he said. "Patrick Riley. Worked on the railroad."

"Did he have a brother named Mike?"

"I believe he did. You couldn't have known him, though. He died years ago, after a life of hard work." He put his thumb on the chain and drew the watch toward him.

"Must not have. Good Irish names, though."

"Oh, yes." He held the watch forward again. "What do you think something like this is worth?"

"I have no idea."

"I've got just a faint one myself, and it's nowhere near the personal value."

"I'm sure."

He put the watch in his pants pocket and brought out a set of brass knuckles. "Here's something that the average fellow might have use for."

"I imagine so. Is this a family heirloom, also?"

"As a matter of fact, it is."

"From your great-uncle Mike, the prizefighter?"

"You're close. He was a policeman. On the streets of New York. He gave this to me when I was a little boy, just before he died."

I was about to tell him what a touching story that was, when the front door opened and a flood of daylight poured in. The brass knuckles went back into Kelly Kelly's pocket, and he leaned on the bar. The daylight closed off, and I watched in the mirror as a newcomer took his place on Kelly's right. I went back to enjoying my beer.

Soon enough, the new customer was hearing the story

of Elwood Johns, the sandstone, and the convict labor. He called for whiskey and seemed to try not to fall into conversation with his neighbor, but within a few minutes Kelly Kelly fetched it out of him that his name was Hibbard and he worked at mining.

He didn't say what kind of mining work he did, but from what I saw in the mirror, he would have been well suited to swinging a pick or pushing an ore cart. He was a big fellow with a thick neck, and the hair below his broad hat brim was close-cropped. When he talked to Kelly Kelly, which was not often, I saw that he had just enough teeth in his mouth to look like a picket fence.

I tried not to watch him, as it seemed to make him watch me in return. I glanced around the tavern, or castle, to see what I might notice. On a ledge behind the bar I saw a row of tumblers like the one Hibbard was drinking from. I recognized them as the kind made of thick glass to give the appearance of more drink for the coin. At the end of the bar to my left, beneath a wall lamp, stood a large glass jar. After glancing at it a few times, I realized it had a rattlesnake coiled inside.

I knew that game, and I didn't play it. A fellow was welcome to bet against the house that he could lay his hand on the glass wall of the jar and not move it when the snake struck out. The bettor had to keep his eye on the jar until the rattler made its strike. I had seen men who claimed to have great willpower and self-control play that game, and I had never seen anyone win.

"Is that right?" rose the voice of Kelly Kelly. "I had an uncle and a great-uncle with the same name. I was just telling Jimmy here about the great-uncle. A policeman on the streets of New York. Hard as iron." He stepped back, and Hibbard looked across at me.

I tipped a nod his way, and he returned the gesture. Then he went back to running a toothpick through the gaps between his teeth.

I succeeded at not watching him for the next several minutes until motion in the mirror caught my eye. First he yawned, so that his mouth looked like a dangerous cavern. Then with one hand he lifted his hat above his head, while with the other he rubbed his almost-bare skull. I was impressed with the size and shape of his head, which was cropped close all over like a jail dock. I had heard of people having their heads shaved and measured, including people who were being held by the law, and I thought this fellow Hibbard might be a good candidate for such a study. Then the head with its lobes and lumps went out of view as the man put the hat on again and looked down at his glass.

I looked around the inside of the tavern some more. Against a side wall, on a shelf about seven feet up, crouched a full mount of a snarling bobcat. On the opposite wall hung a painting of a rider on a rearing horse, with his pistol drawn and pointed at a standing bear. Then, on the wall farthest from me, I saw a wide painting of a train puffing along the side of a deep gorge. I wondered if Mr. Elwood Johns had been an adventurer himself and had a taste for danger, or if he had put up these decorations to give patrons like Kelly Kelly a sense that they, too, were fearless. My glance traveled next to less interesting details, like a dark piano that lay under a coat of dust, and a galvanized tub next to the woodstove, empty except for a few scraps of paper.

Other customers trickled in as I drank my third and fourth beer. Hibbard left the bar and sat by himself at a table. Three rough men who looked like freighters stood at the bar on my left and made short work of a bottle of whiskey. One of them held the bottle upside down and called in a commanding tone to the barkeep, "Empty! Empty!" I saw Hibbard give them an irritated look, and then as he saw me watching him, he raised his eyebrows and looked down at his drink.

As I put one glass of beer after another down the hatch, I began to feel happy and free and far away from worries. Thoughts of Mr. Tull and Mr. Earlywine had vanished, and I was able to ignore most of the people and things in Johns Castle. Time flowed. Once I went out to the latrine, and streaks of daylight still showed. The next time I went out, night had fallen and the sky was dark. Back inside, I saw that someone had taken my place at the bar, so I sat at a table. I thought I should eat something, but I didn't see anyone else eating, and I supposed I would have to go to another place. I didn't want to leave the tavern. I was comfortable there, and girls were starting to show up. If I had had any faint notions, earlier, of gathering more information for the work I was doing for Mr. Tull, those ideas were blotted out. What I wanted to do now was drink, and get close to one of those women with dark plumes and cream-colored bubbies.

Even in my happy state of mind, I didn't try to fool myself about what kind of women they were. To use the polite term, they were soiled doves. Women who exchanged their favors for a price. That was all right with me, because I have a general sympathy for that kind of woman and I think their exchange is fair. Furthermore, I was a long ways from home, where I didn't have any obligations to begin with, and I had some honest wages in my pocket.

Before too long, one of the girls came to stand by my side and lean forward to talk to me. As she did, she showed me a breadth of bosom that made me optimistic.

"What's your name?" she asked.

"Jimmy."

"Mine's Flora."

She had blond hair pinned up in a coil, dark blue eyes, and very light skin. Her features in themselves did not move me, but she had some good spark to her. "Happy to meet you, Flora," I said.

"Are you new in town?"

"I'm just passin' through. How about yourself?"

"I've been here a few months. I was pretty sure I hadn't seen you before."

"Well, you were right. I'm staying over, so I thought I'd stop in here and take it easy for the evening."

"Oh, you ought to." She ran her tongue across her upper lip. "Tell me, Jimmy, are you the kind of gentleman that would buy a girl a drink?"

"That I am. Would you like to sit down?"

"Of course." She pulled a chair next to me and sat down so that her knee touched my leg.

A second barman had come on duty, and he appeared with a small glass of amber liquid for her. I gave him two bits, and he disappeared.

"Here's to it," I said, touching my large glass to her small one. "And to them that can do it."

She made a clever smile and took a sip of whatever was

in her glass. Half a minute later, she leaned forward and put her hand on my leg, as if she needed to do that to get my attention.

"Where are you headed to, Jimmy?"

"Pueblo."

"Oh, that's a nice town. But so is this one." She paused and gave me a full look with her blue eyes. "It depends on what you like, of course."

"I'm easy to please."

"I bet you are." She had lifted her hand from my leg, and now she put it there again.

I was starting to feel bold. "How about yourself?"

"What? Am I easy to please?"

"Well, that, or maybe the other way. Do you make it easy for someone else?"

"I don't know, Jimmy. I haven't been told." She ran her tongue along her upper lip again and patted my leg.

"I bet you know a lot of things without having to be told."

She smiled. "A few."

"You're cute," I said. "I want to tell you a joke."

"Oh, good. I love jokes."

"Well, I heard this one in Spanish, but I think it translates all right."

"Go ahead."

I looked at her full mouth, her bosom, and her exposed ankle. A joke wasn't going to hurt anything. "There was this girl who went to a dance—at a wedding, I think. A fella came up and asked her to dance, and when he rubbed up against her, she asked, 'What's that I feel?' 'Oh, nothing,' he answered. 'I just got paid.' Then another young man asked her to dance, and when they were out on the floor, she felt something similar. She put her hand on it and asked, 'Did you just get paid, too?' 'Yeah,' he said. 'Huh,' she said back. 'I think that boy over there makes more than you do.' "

Flora broke into a laugh. "That's a naughty joke. I like it."

"It was funny when I heard it. And it didn't come out too bad in English."

She touched her knee against my leg again and asked, "So are you traveling by yourself, or do you have someone waiting for you?"

"Oh, no. I'm by myself. No one to answer to." I raised my eyebrows.

"Did you just get paid?"

"It sort of feels like it."

"That's good. Are you the kind of boy that likes to go to the room?"

"I believe so."

She put her hand on my thigh, not too far from my bankroll. "I wouldn't want you to waste the chance."

"Neither would I."

"Do you want to go, then?" She gave me a little nod.

"I don't know. I need to ask a couple of things first, I guess."

Her hand went up to her hair. "Like what?"

"Well, first off, I'd want to have an idea of how much it might be."

"Just five dollars," she said.

That seemed like quite a bit, at first. At my rate of exchange, it was the price of fifty glasses of beer, but if I looked at it another way, it wasn't much more than a fourth of a day's wages, at Mr. Tull's rate. "Do all the girls charge that?" I asked.

"I don't know what the others charge. But that's what I ask."

"Then I suppose a fella gets a good value."

"If you mean quality, of course he does."

When I'm around a woman like that—a saloon girl—and she's the kind for me, there's a feeling I get. It's sort of a ripple inside me. Some girls can play with my leg and lick their lips and do all those cute things, and I can sit and drink my beer and not be moved a bit. But others, like Flora, don't have to do much more than just get close, and they give me the feeling. So I was interested.

"How-all do we do it, then?" I asked.

"Well, we get up and go through that door, and we go to the room."

"I mean, how do things get done once we're there?"

She looked at me serious-like. "Why, normal. I don't do any of those French tricks. I don't have to. It's good with me the regular way."

"I just thought I'd ask. You know, sometimes a fellow gets in the room, and the girl turns kind of stingy on him."

"How do you mean? If she goes to the room, she's gonna do it. That's the point of it, or she couldn't ask for anything."

"What I mean is, sometimes they do things that aren't very inspiring."

"Like what?"

"Like they don't take their dress off."

"It takes a lot of time to take everything off and then get it all back on and in place. It's not like a farm girl who's not wearin' much to begin with, and needs to put things on fast when someone else comes into the barn."

I nodded but went on with my own line. "And the other

thing is, sometimes they don't take their underwear off all the way. They just pull one leg through, and leave the drawers on the other leg. That's not quality to me." The girls I was thinking of also tended to lie there and look away at the corner of the room as if they were waiting for someone to take out the chamber pot, but I didn't say anything about that part.

"I think you can expect more than that when you go with the best," she answered.

"Meanin' you."

"Of course."

"Do you take all your clothes off, then?"

"I don't always. But I will with you."

The boldness came on real fine then, and I said, "I'd like to try the best."

She took me by the hand and said, "You'll see."

I followed her out back of the Castle where there was a row of three or four rooms built in the style of a long lean-to. I had seen the wood structure when I went out to the outhouse, and I hadn't thought much about it. Now I saw its purpose.

She took out a key and opened the door of the second room, or crib. When she lit the lamp I saw that it was a typical room of that kind, meager and spare, with a bed, a dressing table, two chairs, and a foot rug. I asked her if I could help her off with her clothes, and she said it would be all right.

I made a leisurely job out of that part, not wanting to hurry any of the pleasure. When I pulled the top of her dress forward and down, her bubbies bounced out pert and firm in the lamplight, and when I had everything off and draped on a chair, I could see she had a nice figure.

She turned down the lamp and eased onto the bed. I had my clothes shucked in no time, and she had a smile on her face when she took me to her. She went into the action with enthusiasm, I'd say, and there was no problem with her looking away at a corner of the room.

When we were done, I said, "I should come to Cañon City more often."

"I wouldn't complain," she answered.

Back inside the Castle, I stayed on my feet and more or less had my wits about me for another hour or so. I remember seeing Kelly Kelly, who was still holding forth at the bar, and Hibbard, who was drifting here and there. Then I don't remember any more.

I woke up in the chill that comes just before dawn. I was in the alleyway out back, curled up and trying not to get any colder. I stood up, shivering, and checked my pockets. I had the feeling that someone had gone through my wallet, but I didn't seem to have lost anything. I flailed my arms as I went around the building to the main street, and then I took off on a brisk walk to the livery stable.

There I crawled into a bed of straw and pulled my blankets over me. My shivering went away, but my body felt desolate and my head was still pounding. I told myself I needed to get straightened out and tend to business. I was nowhere near being done with my work for Mr. Tull, and I felt his eyes on me as I wallowed in my misery, huddled beneath my blanket. I reminded myself that Doña Dolores used to live in this very town, but I felt too weak and helpless to get any benefit out of being there. On a better day I might have gone out and tried to see things she had seen, and I might have tried to feel her presence in some way.

But today was far from being a good day. I had a feeling of dread flowing in my veins, a dull restlessness that wouldn't let me sleep. At times like that, I have an all-too-close awareness that death comes to the wretched likes of me with no pity and no apology. It's a lonely feeling to be sick at heart for drinking so much and then to lie in such a jangle and not be able to sleep.

The first gray light was creeping into the stable, and I could hear roosters crowing. I tried to put myself to sleep, but all I could do was see images of people I had and hadn't known. They came and went, and after a little while I managed to fall into a light sleep, only to wake every few minutes and tell myself that I had just been dreaming of Mr. Tull, Doña Dolores, or Mr. Earlywine.

Chapter Six

Out on the road again with Cañon City behind me, I still felt wretched. My headache and grogginess seemed way out of proportion to the amount I had drunk or remembered drinking. Sometimes when I felt that terrible I had floating memories of taking slugs of whiskey or tequila and chasing the firewater with beer, but as I thought about the blurry events from the night before, I couldn't recall any heroic hoisting of the bottle. But my head hurt like hell. I wondered if someone had put something in my drink, and if so, why. I also wondered if it had anything to do with the girl.

On the latter point, I didn't think Flora had any part in my current misery. I was feeling light and loose by the time I met her, but I still had my wits about me, and every moment of my interlude with her came back in clear detail. I knew I didn't take a drink with me to the room, and I didn't lose track of things until I had been back in the saloon for a while. In the meanwhile, she hadn't been hovering around me any more. Like most girls of her trade, she ignored a man when she was done with him. I understood that practice, and I could remember she had observed it. So if anyone put anything in my drink, for reasons I still could not fathom, I was sure it wasn't Flora.

I didn't find her a bad one to think back on, as far as that went. She had her pride, and she played an honest game. Of course, she had some appearances to maintain. I assumed that Flora was her summer name and that her original was Ruth or Blanche or something in that line. It occurred to me that she might have taken the name of Flora from the nearby town of Florence, which was my next scheduled stop. There was also a town named Wetmore, and I thought that would be a handy last name for her. Whatever the case, she was a good girl in her own right, and I wouldn't soon forget the sensation of the canyon walls closing in.

I couldn't think of anything for very long, though, without wondering why I felt as if I'd had my snout in a jar of chloroform. Johns Castle wasn't the kind of place where travelers got carried out in the bottom of a dung cart or turned into link sausage. The closest thing to a swindle that I saw was the rattlesnake in a jar, and even that was a fair game to anyone who thought he could win at it.

I rode on without clearing the residue of the night before from my head. Odd impressions kept flitting through my mind in a haphazard sort of way, and Mr. Earlywine kept showing up as if he had something to do with the trip I was undertaking or the bleary state of mind I had brought on. I told myself he was just a dead man and kept coming around because of the morbid poison I felt in my veins, but I still couldn't get rid of him, or Mr. Tull, or the impression I had of Raymond—a sulky young man smoking tailor-made cigarettes, standing beneath a tree on a moonlit night, waiting for something or somebody I had no idea of.

After about an hour on the road, I remembered I was supposed to check for mail in Cañon City. Now I felt guilty and stupid all over again. I was supposed to be doing a job for Mr. Tull, and I had gone drifty. Then, as I was skulking out of town, I had forgotten about Magdalena and the possibility that she might have sent me a letter. To go back would mean a loss of two hours, and even though Mr. Tull wasn't paying me by the hour, I didn't think I would be sticking to my job very well if I got sidetracked by personal business, especially after I had gotten stupefied by personal pleasure.

I stopped the horse and tried to think things through, but I couldn't make up my mind. If I went back, I was loafing on Mr. Tull. If I kept going and missed a letter from Magdalena, it might come to her attention and I would have no reasonable explanation.

Now that I thought of it, I realized I had forgotten about Nena for quite a while. I wondered if I had put her out of my mind so I could frolic with less worry—and if I had done so, I wondered why. There was nothing about my relation with Magdalena that I would compromise or be cheating on if I took a whirl with someone else, and yet I felt guilty. My indulgence with Flora was supposed to be free and open, and it felt that way until I remembered Nena. Somewhere in the bottom of the glass, so to speak, was a residue of the blond girl, Helen, that I had gotten into so much trouble over. I had felt pulled to her like a far-gone drunkard is pulled to drink. When I thought of Magdalena, I remembered this other girl that Nena had known about and had encouraged me to get loose from.

Now I wondered if, in a way, my tumble with Flora was an attempt at having something to do with Helen again. I didn't think so, but everything was so jumbled that I felt I had failed someone, mainly Nena, and in some way that went beyond forgetting to check for a letter.

After several minutes of hemming and hawing, I decided to throw away the two hours it would take me to backtrack and make things right, at least with myself. So I turned the tall horse around and headed west.

I hadn't gone but half a mile when I came up over a rise and saw a horse and rider coming my way. I felt a jolt of worry right away, as I had the feeling in the pit of my stomach that this other person was following me. When he stopped, my feeling got stronger, as I imagined he had not expected me to turn around.

I rode down the slope toward him, and he put his horse into motion and then stopped again, as if on second thought. As I rode closer to him, I noticed the broad-brimmed hat and the close-cropped head that looked no softer or smoother than a turnip. From a hundred yards away I could identify my fellow traveler as none other than the surly Mr. Hibbard from the night before.

He didn't move his horse again during the time I rode toward him. I didn't know if he wanted to pretend he wasn't following me or if he thought that by making me come to him he would have some control over the meeting. Either way, there was no avoiding me. I rode up to within a few yards of him and spoke.

"Mr. Hibbard, isn't it?"

"None other."

I could see his hard features in the shade of his hat brim. I thought he was trying to intimidate me, but I felt I had to speak up for myself. "I didn't know you were on my back trail," I said, "or I would have turned around sooner."

"A man's got a right to travel where he wants."

"No doubt. I wouldn't think to question you."

"Wouldn't do much good." His jaw muscles bulged.

"But in case you're interested, I'm goin' back to Cañon City now. I've had my morning ride, and I'm going back to town."

"Suit yourself. But what makes you think I care?"

"In case you wanted to follow me some more."

He spit tobacco juice off to the side, and as he turned to speak I could see his picket fence of teeth. "You've got a lot of smart talk, fella. I took enough of it last night, and I don't need to take any more. And don't think you're so important that someone would want to follow you."

I gave him a close look. "I don't know what you mean about last night. I hardly spoke to you."

He spit again. "As far as you remember, maybe. You got drunk as an Indian and shot off your mouth, and I didn't think it'd be fair to clean someone's plow when he was that drunk. But if you keep it up today, I won't go so easy on you."

I didn't have much answer for that because I couldn't remember the tail end of the evening, but I was pretty sure he was just bluffing to shift the subject. Finally, I thought of something to say.

"You don't need to make yourself sound so generous. It's not enough to make me think you weren't following me."

"By God," he said as he swung down from his horse. "Get down, and I'll pound you."

I didn't feel like fighting at all, but if I wanted to save face with this fellow I didn't have much choice. So I let myself down from the tall horse and set my hat on the saddle horn.

He stepped up to me, cocked his right fist and fluttered it, and then came around with a left that put me on the ground with a thud. The two jolts were so close together that I couldn't gather my thoughts right away.

"That was too easy," he said, standing over me. "Maybe it's enough to give you the idea. Just stay out of my way." He climbed back into the saddle and rode away to the east.

I rolled over to all fours and pushed myself up onto my feet. My horse had shied away but my hat was still on the saddle horn, so I walked straight at him, keeping my eye on his shoulder in front of the saddle, and gathered up the reins.

Left-handed, I thought. That was how he got to me. If I ever ran into him again, which I hoped I didn't, I would have to remember that.

The trip to Cañon City and back turned out to be fruitless. All the way there, I reminded myself that I told Magdalena I would check the mail in Cañon City and Florence. If she wrote to me at only one place, I wouldn't want to miss the letter, and even if she didn't write at all, it was a matter of honor that I did what I said I would. When I found no mail at last in Cañon City, I headed back toward Pueblo, by way of Florence. I told myself all I was out was two hours, plus a punch on the side of my head, and I had made good on my word.

At least I didn't have anyone on my trail any longer, as nearly as I could see. I rode past the spot of our scuffle, without stopping, and came into the main street of Florence in the early afternoon. For all I knew, Hibbard was holed up someplace watching to see if I was riding through. I couldn't let that stop me, though.

What did cause me to drop anchor was a letter, written on a single piece of paper and folded into the shape of an envelope, which I found waiting for me in the post office. It was from Magdalena, and it said she was right there in Florence, staying for two days at a guesthouse called the Four Roses. The letter was dated the day before. I assumed her lodging place was not the kind of hotel that would have its own stationery or a big sign on Main Street, so I asked the fellow behind the wicket in the post office where it was. He told me how to find the place, so I walked back out into the bright day.

I found the Four Roses on a side street. It occupied a two-story wood building, clean and modest, facing east. It looked like the kind of place that let rooms by the day, week, or month and did not serve meals. Once inside, as the tinkling of the doorbell faded, I found myself in a small front room with a registration desk and a sitting area big enough for two wooden chairs. A lady with a pinched face and sunken mouth appeared at the counter. When I asked for Magdalena Lozano, the woman told me to have a seat and she would go tell her.

A few minutes later, Nena came into the room through a different door than the one the landlady had used.

"Hola, Yimi," she said, smiling. *"¿Cómo estás?"* She was wearing a plain, dark cotton dress that showed her figure to advantage, as usual. Her red lipstick matched a pair of small earrings that might have been rubies or garnets. She had a relaxed, happy expression on her face, and her green eyes were shining. She gave me her hand, and then

we both sat down. I felt nervous and still a bit hazy, but deep down I knew I was in the right company.

I spoke to her in Spanish, as usual. "I was surprised to find you here in this town," I said. "I didn't find a letter in Cañon City, and the most I expected here was something in the mail. What a surprise."

"I barely arrived yesterday, and I wrote a letter to both places."

The pinched-face lady appeared again and stayed long enough to see what we were up to, and then she went back into her quarters.

"I suppose the letter hadn't arrived yet when I passed through there."

"Well enough. At least you found me here."

"Yes. And what news do you have for me? I thought you would be in Colorado Springs."

"Well, it turns out that I have to go to Rancho Alegre."

"Oh, I see. And this is on the way?"

"Yes. What happens is, I'm going for Rosa Linda."

"To bring her back?"

"To accompany her, yes. My cousin, her brother, was going to go for her, but he can't go right now. In the family they think she should come back to see my grandmother, and it was decided that I could go for her so that she wouldn't have to travel alone."

"That's good," I said, using a phrase that a person dropped in to ratify any little thing that seemed reasonable. It occurred to me that the family saw quite a difference between Magdalena, who could travel alone, and Rosa Linda, who could not. But I didn't comment on it, of course.

"I thought I would stay here for a while," she said, "because I didn't think I would be in Colorado Esprín when you went by that way."

"As it turns out, I'm not going through there right now. I'm on my way to Pueblo."

"Oh, really?"

"Yes. It seems that the lost son I am looking for has gone to Pueblo to live. I plan to look for him there."

"Oh, that's good."

"And from the look of things, I will probably go back to the north before you do. I have to give my report to the older man, you know."

"Ah, yes. Then this will probably be the only time we see each other on this trip. It's too bad you can't meet my family in Esprín."

"Maybe another time."

"Certainly."

"I wish we had more time," I said, giving her an open smile. "You could go to Pueblo with me, I could go to Rancho Alegre with you, and we could all go back to Espreen together."

"Yes, it would be nice. But this is as much time as I can spare, stopping here. And besides, it's not convenient for me to go to Pueblo."

"I understand."

"And your trip so far, Yimi? It has been good?"

"Oh, yes. I've seen pretty landscapes, and most of the people I met have treated me well." I thought that was cutting it close enough.

"And the mother of the boy? Did you meet her?"

"Unfortunately, she is no longer living."

Nena gave a look of sympathy. “That’s too bad.”

“Yes, it is. I had the impression she was a nice lady. But she has passed on, and her husband as well, so it is only the son I have to look for.”

“I see. Well, I hope you find him.”

“So do I.”

We sat without talking for a few seconds until I thought of something to say. “And everyone back in the town? Your aunt and your uncle, they’re all right?”

“Oh, yes.”

“And your cousin Quico?”

“Also fine.”

“That’s good. Any other news?”

She gave a thoughtful look and shook her head.

“Did you hear, by chance, about a man who died just before I left town?”

“Oh, yes. Over there on the other side. Someone killed him, wasn’t it? Poor man.”

“Yes. I don’t remember if I told you this. He wanted me to do some work for him, too, but the idea didn’t set well with me, so I took this other work instead.”

“No, you didn’t tell me that part, but that’s all right. I think it’s better what you do, to help a man find his son, although I don’t know what the other work was like.”

I wrinkled my nose. “It was nothing important—not to me, at least. And it seemed like trouble. Then, when I found him dead, I was convinced it was not good.”

“Oh, you found him?”

“Yes, I went back to tell him I had other work, but when I went to his house, he was already dead.”

“Poor man.”

"Yes. But there was nothing I could do about it. I couldn't change anything, not even my having met him, much less my finding him like that."

"That's true. Once a chicken's throat has been cut, you can't get the blood back into the veins."

I took her remark to refer to my dealings with Mr. Earlywine and his death in general, not the actual bloodshed. In point of fact, he had been shot in the head and hadn't bled that much anyway.

"That's right," I said. "And I had to talk to the sheriff and explain how it came to pass that I found a murdered man."

"That's too bad."

"Yes, and for that reason I was wondering whether anyone had found out any more about it."

She shook her head like before. "Not that I know of. But let's hope they find out. It's not good that things of that nature don't get solved."

"Well," I said, making a motion with my hand as if to brush away the unpleasantness, "all of that is far away, and we have other things to tend to. You have your cousin, and I have the lost son."

"Yes. Do you stay here tonight, in Florence?"

I felt a bit of disappointment as I shook my head. "I don't think so. I feel that I'm behind, or running late, as it is. And yourself?"

"To begin with, I was going to stay two nights here, but now it seems to be early enough that I might be able to make it to the rancho before nightfall. But they are not expecting me until tomorrow, and I already have the room paid."

"Oh."

"But you're in a hurry."

"Not really. I just hadn't thought about spending the night here." As I had never spent the night with her, or done anything close to it, I didn't think I was in danger of passing up an opportunity. And the prospect of mounting the stairs in the pinched-face woman's establishment struck me as pretty distant.

"If you're not in a hurry, and I don't have to go anywhere until tomorrow, maybe we could go out to find something to eat. Are you hungry?" Her face had brightened, and her eyes were shining.

"Just like always. And I would be happy to invite you." My nervousness had faded, and I was feeling the charm of her presence.

"Well, I invited," she answered.

I shook my head. "The old man has paid me well."

"I have my grandmother's money," she said with a smile.

"Hang on to it. I'm enchanted with the idea of inviting you."

I left Florence feeling much better than I had felt earlier in the day, thanks to a good meal and the company of a pretty girl. My headache had lifted, and most of the dread feeling had gone out of my body. As I went to the café and back with Magdalena, I wondered if anyone was watching me. I thought that if there was, I didn't mind being seen in such good company, but I didn't like the idea that someone might then have a reason to keep an eye on her. For that reason only, I thought it was just as well that we parted with only a touch of the hand. After I left her in the front room of the Four Roses, I walked my horse out onto the main street and headed east, still on foot.

I paused to chat in Spanish with a *chavalo* who was cleaning a wrought-iron gate in front of a large house. The lad told me that his *patrón* was a good man, that he made much money in mining, horses, cattle, and land. The *patrón,* poor fellow who sneezed much because of the dust, still wanted to buy an automobile. At my asking, the *chavalo* smiled and said he would love to learn how to drive such a machine. As I talked to the lad, I took the opportunity to glance up and down the street. I saw nothing but the slow movements of a drowsy, dusty town. After complimenting the *chavalo* on the good work he was doing, I hoisted myself up into the saddle and went on my way.

As the tall horse stepped along and I thought ahead about getting to Pueblo, I turned over Magdalena's comment about it not being convenient for her to go to that town. Sometimes when I'm off on my own I like to play a word or phrase through my mind a few times. Sometimes it's just a set of smooth sounds, like "Cuervo Azul" or "Rancho Alegre," but at others it's an expression that I pick apart for meaning. I could remember Magdalena's words: *"No me conviene ir a Pueblo."* I had taken it to mean that it was not convenient for her. Now, as I was out on the trail and mulled it over, I realized she might have meant that it wasn't good for her, or advisable, to go to Pueblo. I thought of that meaning because I had been told once, by an older and more cautious man, that it was not convenient, or advisable, for me to go to a murky establishment that I thought might be quite to my liking. Whatever Magdalena's primary meaning was, I would have to wait to see how it came around.

At the edge of town I saw a dark-haired little white boy,

maybe six years old, chasing chickens around the yard and waving a stick at them. A woman who looked almost old enough to be his grandmother but who was probably his mother called out in a shrill voice.

"Leave off chasin' the hens, Sonny, for if you kill one, yer fahther'll tan yer hide."

The little boy said something I didn't catch, and the woman called back, "Never you mind. If he wants to kill one, that's up to him."

I rode on, glad once more to be free of chickens in my life. But the incident made me think of Mr. Earlywine, by way of Magdalena's comment about not being able to get the blood back into a chicken's veins. She was sure right about that. A person couldn't change what had happened. I knew that from the time I had had a chicken foot in my mouth. Take it out as discreetly as I could, I could not say it hadn't been there, and I could not look around and say for certain that I was alone.

Chapter Seven

On the outskirts of Pueblo, I swung down from the horse to water some cactus and stretch my arms and legs. I had rolled out of my blankets early that morning and had kept a steady pace until I came to this high spot, where I could see the town south and east of me. Straight south about a mile, I could make out a crew of men, horses, and mules working on some kind of a roadbed. The teams were pulling scrapers and floats, and the men were milling around like so many dark ants. It was a warm afternoon like the one before, so I sat in the shade of the horse for a few minutes and watched the workers in the distance.

Sometimes it seemed as if the world was full of industry, like the road-building down below me and the smokestacks rising out of the town a ways farther off. At other times, though, it seemed as if the world was full of drifters and loafers and opportunists. I had a hunch that Raymond Bowden was one of the latter group and wouldn't be found in a work crew, getting browned by the sun and wind. That was just a hunch, though, and I would begin to know more when I found his friend Mr. Jeffrey.

Not having been to Pueblo before, I was surprised to see what a sophisticated little city it was. Not only did it have elegant houses of brick and red sandstone, but it had a new three-story train depot. Downtown, the larger buildings ran to two, three, and four stories of stone and brick. On the street corners, some of the nicer buildings had rounded edges while some had the corners shaved off diagonally. It was obvious to me that some people took care to build things that were long-lasting and pleasing to the eye. Even the saloons and brothels, which I picked out with little effort, spent something on appearances.

I found a place called the Silver Cloud, where the beer was cold and the barkeep friendly. After some casual talk about the beauty of his city, I told him I was looking for a man named Jeffrey. He told me I might look up a fellow named Arthur Jeffrey, who had some kind of hand in the mining business. That didn't surprise me, as it seemed that plenty of men down this way had something to do with mining coal, ore, or precious metals. Under the general rule that a fellow didn't need to tell all his business, I thought it might be better if I didn't mention Raymond. So I thanked the barkeep for his information on Mr. Jeffrey and stayed long enough to be polite.

Fortified by two glasses of cold beer, I made my way back out into the sunny afternoon and climbed into the saddle. The tall horse never seemed to mind whether we were in town, out on the open plains, or on a steep mountain trail. Pueblo had its share of noise, with steam engines and whistles and blasts of air, interspersed with sounds of thumping and crushing, but the horse just clomped along unbothered. About ten blocks north of the Silver Cloud, following the barkeep's instructions, I found a low building with a shingle of a sign that read "A. Jeffrey."

I swung down, tied my horse, and then climbed up onto the board sidewalk. As I approached the office door and looked through the pane of glass, I saw a long-faced man sitting at an oak desk. He was resting his chin in both hands, and he had his elbows on top of the desk. He held his gaze straight ahead, not quite at the door, and he looked as if he had been in the pose for a while. As I opened the door and walked in, he lifted his head in a slow movement and looked at me.

He had an unpleasant expression on his face, worse than sadness. The area below his eyes hung slack and wrinkly. His hair, thinning on top, hung in brown wisps over his ears. I would guess him to be somewhere in the range of forty to fifty years old, and he did not look as if he had enjoyed much of his life so far or expected to do so in the future.

I took off my hat. "Good afternoon," I said, trying to put a cheery tone in the air.

He made a dip of the head that passed for a nod, and then in a tired voice he said, "What do you need?"

"I'm looking for a Mr. Jeffrey, and I'm not sure if this is the right place."

"Depends on which one you're lookin' for."

"A Mr. Arthur Jeffrey."

"He ain't here." The man turned down the corners of his mouth and made his face look longer, if possible.

"Well, maybe you can help me."

Long Face gave me a stare that said maybe he could and maybe he didn't care.

Still trying to keep up some spirit, I said, "I'm actually looking for someone else, and I understand I might be able to find him through his friend, Mr. Jeffrey."

Long Face glanced to his right, where another desk, darker than his and with a shelf of pigeonholes, sat against the wall. "Like I say, he ain't here."

I looked at the desk, which had stacks of papers heaped on it. On the left end of it, hanging from a hook, was a short chain of two links with a key attached.

"Maybe you can help me," I said again. "The person I'm looking for is named Raymond Bowden, and they told me in his hometown that he had a friend here in Pueblo named Mr. Jeffrey."

Long Face lifted his face about an inch. "I can't answer for his friends or his personal business. This is an office that deals with mining claims."

"I see. And when do you think I could hope to ask Mr. Jeffrey in person?"

"I can't speak for that."

"Today, perhaps?"

"It's his office. He comes and goes as he wishes."

I took a deliberate breath. "As well he should. But do you think it would be worth my while to come back in, say, an hour?"

"Suit yourself."

Taking that to mean something other than "No," I said, "Thank you. I think I'll call back then." I turned and walked to the door, putting on my hat. When I had gone out and was closing the door behind me, I glanced back.

Long Face had settled his head onto the heels of his hands again and had resumed his vacant gaze.

I rode my horse around the block and came up through the alley. Counting the buildings and noting their size, I figured out which one held Mr. Jeffrey's office. In back of it, by the alley, sat a stable with a chain and padlock on the door. That didn't tell me much, except that Long Face probably came and went through the front door. Maybe Mr. Jeffrey did, too.

With an hour to kill and no great need to drink any more beer, although the idea presented itself, I decided to ride around and reinforce my sense of how the town was laid out. I rode back down Main Street, noticed the Silver Cloud, and located the avenue that came in from the train station. Then I rode back toward Mr. Jeffrey's office, taking a street that ran parallel to Main Street and then going back and forth on cross streets to get an idea of what this part of town looked like.

A few people were out on the street, here and there, most of them keeping to the shady side. In my wandering I crossed Mr. Jeffrey's street a few times and could see his office in the middle of the block, facing south. Nothing moved in front of the office until, on one of my crossings, I saw a man with a tube of rolled-up paper open the door and go in.

I waited a couple of minutes and then rode down the block. I tied my horse in front of the building next door, stepped up onto the sidewalk, and moved to the door of Mr. Jeffrey's office.

Through the pane I could see the man with the rolled-up paper standing between the two desks. Long Face was standing behind his own desk and was putting on a short-billed cap. I thumped a boot heel on the sidewalk, then opened the door and walked in.

"This is him here," said Long Face, pointing a thumb in my direction.

"Oh, I see." A man with reddish-brown hair and an automatic smile turned to look at me. Then he turned to his clerk and said, "Good enough, then."

Long Face muttered, "See you on Monday," and headed for the door.

By now I had my hat in my hand, and I moved aside to let him pass. Then I turned to greet the other man.

"Mr. Jeffrey?"

"I sure am. And how can I help you?" His gray eyes gave me a quick looking-over.

"I'm trying to find a young man named Raymond Bowden. Some people in Paloma Springs told me he had come here to Pueblo and had a friend named Mr. Jeffrey. I was wondering if you might be the man."

"Oh, yes. Raymond." The man gave a light laugh. "I see him once in a while."

I glanced around the office. "He doesn't work here, then."

"Oh, no."

"I don't mean to be too inquisitive, but I didn't get much to go on, and I didn't know if he worked with you."

"Not really." Mr. Jeffrey put on his smile again. "I'm in a special kind of business. I work with mining claims."

"Buying and selling them?"

"Something like that. Of course, a great deal of it is confidential, and I can't talk much about it."

"Of course. I gather that your work takes you away quite a bit."

"Like I say, I can't say."

I tipped him a brisk nod. "Oh, certainly. All I meant was, I understood why you might not see Raymond very often."

"Oh, one thing and another." He gave his light laugh again.

"Do you have any idea of where I might find him? An address, perhaps?"

His eyebrows went up as his mouth opened. "Oh, I couldn't say that I know that much."

"I see. He doesn't live with you, then."

Mr. Jeffrey shook his head. "Oh, no. It's been a while since he was a guest at my house. Not that he wouldn't be welcome again, you understand, but he goes where he pleases." Then came the full smile.

"I see." I glanced at Long Face's empty desk and at the dark, cluttered desk with the key hanging on it. Then my eyes met Mr. Jeffrey's. "Do you have any idea where he might be of late?"

He tapped the tube of paper against his free hand. "You know, it just so happens that I might be able to help you there. I talked to a mutual friend of ours just a day or two ago, and he told me Raymond was out at the McMasters ranch."

"Working?"

"Oh, I don't think so."

"Just staying there, then, or in some kind of a business capacity?"

"Raymond has friends everywhere. But, of course, if he has an eye out for an opportunity—well, who wouldn't?"

"Naturally."

Mr. Jeffrey gave me a sincere nod at that point. "And yourself? I don't believe I caught your name."

"Jimmy Clevis." I held out my hand.

"Arthur Jeffrey," he answered as he offered me his hand. Then the gray eyes held me. "And where are you from, Jimmy?"

My inner voice whispered caution. "Most recently I came from Grand Junction," I said. "I was in North Platte before that, and I expect to end up in Amarillo."

"Quite a loop."

"It sure is." I gave him a moment to hope for more information, and then I said, "It seems that Raymond's father, Mr. Bowden, had a few interests in one place and another, and there might be some expectations for Raymond."

Mr. Jeffrey tilted his head. "I'm sure he'll be glad to know of it."

"Oh, I'm sure. But I've probably said more than I should. Confidential, you know." I tapped the side of my cheek.

"Indeed I do."

I waited for him to say more, but he didn't, so I took up the thread. "I suppose, then, that I should go on out to the McMasters ranch. Could you give me an idea of how to get there?"

"Certainly. It's west and south from here."

"Out towards Wetmore?"

"In that direction. You'll come to a little settlement out there called Siloam, and the McMasters place is south of that."

"Good ranch country?"

"Oh, yes. Are you riding?"

"I sure am."

"You'll find it all good to look at. I'd guess you have a good eye for cattle and horses." He put his free thumb in his waistcoat and squared his shoulders back, and I noticed his watch chain.

"I might. I know the feel of a horse under me, and I've seen the south end of a lot of cattle." Our conversation seemed to have ended, so I said, "I suppose I should be going. Thank you for all your help."

"My pleasure."

He held out his hand, and we shook again. Then, as I turned toward the door, he caught me with a question.

"By the way, Jimmy, what was Mr. Bowden's first name? Raymond's father, that is. I can't for the life of me remember it, though I met him several times."

I felt a chill in my blood, but I made a quick recovery as I turned around. "Philip," I answered. "Though not everyone called him that."

"That's right," he said. "Philip."

"And the late Mrs. Bowden was Dolores."

"Oh, yes. The best of women."

I made a solemn nod and reached for the door handle. "Well, thanks again."

"Any time. And good luck."

"Thank you, and the same to you."

Out on the street, I gathered my reins and stepped up into the saddle. I imagined I had a twenty-mile ride ahead of me, at the least, to get to the McMasters place. I wondered if Raymond had really been out that way or if his friend Jeffrey was sending me on a wild-goose chase. I didn't think I had much choice, though. I had to follow up on it, and even if Raymond wasn't there, I might learn more about him.

Rather than ride straight out of town, I decided to come back around the block in five or ten minutes to see if anything interesting presented itself. So I rode over to Main Street, went south a couple of blocks, and then turned west. Two blocks later I turned north, then zigzagged a couple of more times, rode within a block of Jeffrey's office, and paused at the alleyway that ran in back. I thought of the two-link chain and key I had seen in the office and of the padlock I had seen on the stable. I doubted that Jeffrey had Raymond cached in the building out back, but my basic judgment told me this fellow had something to hide, and men of his cut were as familiar with alleys and back buildings as I was. So I turned in, riding past a heap of cans and bottles I hadn't noticed before, and keeping an eye on a bumblebee that was zooming toward and away from a stand of hollyhocks.

I heard a noise up ahead of me. It sounded like a door opening, and it made me not want to be seen riding down that alley. So I did an about-face and came back out onto the street and turned left. As I did so, I saw something that made me stop short.

Across the street and down a ways, standing on the corner, was a man in a familiar broad-brimmed hat. My stomach lurched as I recognized the hat, the lumpy head, and the husky profile of Hibbard. At the sight of me, he sank back, turned, and walked away.

Now I was convinced that my earlier meeting with Hibbard, and maybe the one before that, was more than coincidence. I didn't think he was out to do me any real harm, or he would have done it when he had the chance. I figured he either wanted to find out what kind of an errand I was on, or he wanted me to lead him to my object. Either way, I didn't like being followed, so I took advantage of his retreat and headed straight south. At the edge of town I circled back a couple of blocks, and seeing no one on my tail, I struck for the open country.

I came to a place where two men with axes were making firewood out of an old corral. I asked them where I could find the road to Wetmore and Siloam, and they pointed me back to the north and west. I cut across the rolling country until I came to the road, a well-traveled one by the looks of it.

With the river not far to the north, I headed mostly westward, going through some large gulches and crossing a couple of creeks. Then I came out on higher grassland, where the country opened up all around and I could see I wasn't being followed. The image of Hibbard slinking back like a deer into a cornfield was all too clear for me.

I let the horse settle into a fast walk and began to think about where I was going to spend the night. I had been sleeping on the ground right regular, so I wasn't worried about comfort. I just wanted a place where I could keep to myself, out of the way, and be able to tell if someone was riding up on me.

I decided to circle back to the last big gulch I had ridden through. When I came to it I struck the creek and followed it upstream, to the southeast, for about half a mile. There I found a spot where I could picket the horse, roll out my blankets, and be glad to have everything at a distance. Again I told myself that if Hibbard had wanted to do me some harm he would have done it already, but I didn't like someone using me for a bird dog.

Morning came on calm and peaceful. When I woke up, the sun was in my eyes. The horse was moving around on his picket rope, and a hawk was floating in the sky above. I got a little fire going, boiled some coffee in a can, and then took the horse to water. By the time I had my camp rolled up and the horse saddled, the sun was warm on my back.

Out on the trail again, I came to the grassland I had reached the evening before. I let the horse fall into a brisk walk, and I tried to imagine how long it would be until I came to this place called Siloam. The road still ran mostly westward. Mountains rose in the distance ahead of me and around to the south as well. I had understood that Siloam was closer than Wetmore, which was at the edge of the mountains, but it was hard to judge distances in country like this, and any buildings I saw were just light-colored specks.

Somewhere along the middle of the morning, I came upon a grizzled old fellow who had his horse tethered to a juniper bush as he sat with his saddle in his lap.

"What, ho," I said as I came to a stop. "Do you need a hand?"

"Not at all," came the answer in a creaky voice.

His saddle looked worn and tattered, so I asked, "Did your outfit come apart on you?"

"Stirrup tried to come off, is all. Don't stop me for long."

"I see." He had a hunting knife poked into the stirrup leather and was boring a hole just the way I had been told not to. "By the way," I said, leaning on the saddle horn with both hands, "could you tell me where this road leads to?"

He looked up with a set of eyes that were yellow with brown centers. "It goes to Wetmore, and from there you can take it through Hardscrabble Canyon and all the way down to Taos if ya want. That's the way Kit Carson and the old-timers used to go, down through San Luis." His eyes slid over me and my horse. "You don't look like you're aimin' to go that far."

"No, I'm not. I'm just tryin' to get the lay of the land this side of Wetmore, get an idea where some of the ranches are."

"Depends on which ones." He gave a twist to the knife, lifted up the leather, and blew crumbs out of it. "Southwest of here there's a few."

"How about west and a ways north, where I see those trees? That looks like a ranch."

"Ah, it's just a Mexican ranch."

"Oh, uh-huh."

He gave me another close look. "You lookin' fer work?"

"No, I'm actually lookin' for a place called the McMasters ranch."

He pointed with the knife over his right shoulder. "It's back thataway. You'll come to a little place called Siloam, and it's south of there."

"That's what I understood, but I thought I'd ask to make sure."

He wrinkled his nose, and his beard went up and down. "You new to the country?"

"Just to this part."

"Well, you have to try pretty hard to git lost along here."

"Uh-huh." I looked again toward the north and west. "You say that's a Mexican ranch over there?"

"That's right. But I don't think you'll find any work there."

I stood in my stirrups to see if I could get a better view. "I'm not lookin' for work. What's the name of that place, do you know?"

"The Mexicans call it Rancho Alegre."

I felt a happy jump in my pulse. "I've heard of that place," I said. "I think I've got time to stop there on my way."

He looked down his nose at the leather. "I hope you git along with greasers, then, 'cause that's all you'll find there."

"I get along with 'em fine. You sure you don't need a hand?"

He gave me a look of disgust, which I took to mean he didn't need a pup like me to fix his outfit.

"Good enough," I said. "Good luck."

He nodded at me, not unfriendly. "You, too."

He bent to his work again, and I turned the tall horse across country toward Rancho Alegre.

Chapter Eight

As I rode up to the rancho where it sat in a grove of cottonwoods, I could see it was laid out in true Mexican style. Somewhat in the style of the old haciendas, but smaller, it had a broad, high wall facing anybody who approached it. In the middle of the wall was a heavy double door, or *portón,* as it was called. The two halves would swing out and make an opening big enough to drive a carriage or wagon through, and when both halves were closed, the one on the left had a walk-through door for anyone on foot or leading a horse. The whole façade, or *fachada* as the Mexicans called it, was plastered and whitewashed, with a row of grated windows along the wall on each side of the *portón.* I could see corrals on the left end, with a large hinged gate, so I imagined buggies and wagons and horseback riders—not to mention cattle and sheep and goats—went in that way as well.

No horses were tied to the hitch rack outside, but as I approached the *portón,* which had its walk-through door half open, I heard voices and light laughter on the other side. The day being Sunday, I imagined visitors would be dropping in—especially if Magdalena and Rosa Linda were here, along with any young women who lived at the rancho. I knew it was nothing to some of these young fellows to ride twenty or thirty miles, sit around and chat and flirt till the party ended, and ride back to catch a few winks before they had to roll out on Monday morning.

I tied my horse to the hitch rack and walked toward the half-open door. Just as I was deciding whether to knock or look in, a medium-sized man with gray hair and a full mustache pushed the door open and raised his hand in greeting.

"Buenas tardes," I said, not sure that it was afternoon but not thinking I should call it morning, either.

His face took on a comfortable look as he saw that we could continue in Spanish. "How may I help you?" he asked.

"I was passing by, and I remembered that a friend of mine was staying here, so I dropped in to say hello to her."

"Very well. And what is the name of the friend?"

"Her name is Magdalena Lozano. She is here, I believe, with her cousin, Rosa Linda."

"Oh, yes. The girls. Very well. I will tell them you are here."

He left me standing at the doorway, but he didn't close it, so I could hear the voices and laughter. I could also smell food, which is always a good omen for me. I couldn't be sure, but I thought I detected the aroma, as the Mexicans say, of roasted pork.

Then I heard Magdalena's voice, lilting in a tone that sounded as if she was talking to another woman. The door opened a little more, and there she stood.

"Yimi! How nice! Don Alvino told me there was a

'gringo' here to see me, and I thought it might be you. But I asked Rosa Linda to look first. You never know." She held out her hand. "But come on in. Today there is a fiesta. There are many people here."

I took her hand, and she led me through the door into a *portal,* a roofed-over entryway between the two sets of rooms I had seen from the outside. The *portal* was a comfortable place, some fifteen feet by twenty, and open on the fourth side, where it looked out on a large back yard area. A canvas canopy was set up, and beneath it were two rows of tables and benches as well as several chairs. A half-dozen men, mainly of middle age, sat in a semicircle at one end of the tables, and a smaller group of younger men sat at the other end. I could hear women's voices coming through an open door on my left, where the smell of roasting green chile came drifting out.

"And Rosa Linda?" I asked, looking at the door that led into the kitchen.

"She'll be right back to say hello. She went to wash her hands."

I turned and got an appreciative look at Nena. She was wearing a tan dress, which set off her dark hair and red lipstick with a rich contrast. "I'm glad to find you here," I said. "I didn't know if you had left yet."

"No, we go tomorrow. We stayed for the fiesta."

"That's good."

"And you? Did you finish your work?"

From the wording of the question I understood that I didn't have to talk about my personal business in detail. "Not yet," I said. "I was on my way to another ranch when it occurred to me that I could pass by here and say hello."

"How nice. And here is Rosa Linda."

It finally occurred to me to take off my hat as I turned and gave my hand to the pretty cousin. "Good afternoon. It is a pleasure to see you again."

"Likewise. And welcome to Rancho Alegre."

"Thank you." I took a quick look at Rosa Linda. She hadn't changed since the previous two times I had met her. Her hair came halfway to her shoulders and her complexion was a light tan. She had an open smile and a radiant expression. All in all, she looked innocent and spotless in her bright yellow dress. I thought again of that time, a while back, when Magdalena asked me if I was interested in her cousin. Now even more than before, I thought she was far too clean to have much to do with the likes of me. But I was happy to be at the same party with her.

I thought of the old codger I had seen on the side of the trail, doing violence to the stirrup leather, and I recalled his warning that all I would find here would be Mexicans. In my present company, I sure couldn't see anything wrong with it. It was just as well, though, that a lot of gringos felt that way. There was enough competition as things were.

I turned to Magdalena. "I know you weren't expecting me," I said, "so if you have things to tend to . . ." I made a motion with my hat, as if I was getting ready to be on my way.

"Oh, no," she said. "Come and sit down. There will be food in a little while. And something to drink. You would like that?"

"I'm sure I would. I have to arrive at the other ranch sometime today, but I am not in a hurry."

"Do they expect you?"

"No, not really."

Magdalena's eyes sparkled. "Well, then, enjoy the fiesta a little. Eat something, drink something, meet some people. Enjoy it."

Rosa Linda spoke up. "You attend to Yimi, Nena, and I'll go back to the kitchen. Don't worry. There are many hands to do the work."

"That's fine," said Magdalena. "Thank you." Then she turned to me and held out her hand. "Come, Yimi. I will introduce you, so that you may enjoy the party in confidence."

I was familiar with their idea of confidence, which meant to go ahead and feel comfortable, so I nodded and stepped toward her. I felt another spark as I let her take me by the hand and lead me in the direction of the other guests.

"These are good people," she said. "They come from many places, but they are all decent. Don Alvino does not invite lowly types."

I thought of myself, who was uninvited. I hadn't had a bath in over a week, and I was sure I looked it. I didn't want to contradict her by using myself as an example, but it did occur to me that if an unscrubbed fellow like me could get in the gate, Don Alvino's standards were not as hard as iron.

A human form came up to us out of nowhere, it seemed. It was a short man, probably no older than myself, but balding and soft-bellied. He had a wispy beard and stringy hair, thick lips, a button nose, and a pair of spectacles. He looked as if he might be half Mexican, and it was anyone's guess what the other half might be.

He gave a simpering smile and said to Magdalena, in halting Spanish, "I hope you have time to sit with us. We are enchanted by the pretty girl."

"My cousin?"

"No. You yourself."

"How nice, Rogelio. We are going there."

I nodded at him, but he ignored me as he bowed to her and turned away. He had a funny walk, uneven and limping-like, and I imagined it had something to do with his swayback and belly. "He likes you," I said.

Magdalena heaved out a breath and looked up at her eyebrows. *"Ay. A mí me repugna y a Rosa Linda también."* He is repugnant to me and to Rosa Linda as well.

I saw that Rogelio, or Repugno as I thought to call him, was taking a chair with the group of young men. "Do we go with them?" I asked.

"I imagine so," she said. "For a little while."

Repugno made a show of setting a chair in place for Magdalena, and another of the young men positioned a chair for me. Before I sat down, I was introduced to all four and shook hands with each of them—Carlos, Alejandro, Ramón, and Rogelio. The other three were all clean, idle-looking fellows, pleasant and polite but not showing any evidence of hard work or deep thought. The one named Alejandro looked the softest, though he wasn't fat, and he had the handshake of a plump old lady. The young men spoke Spanish among them, the other three being much better at it than Rogelio, but all four of them spoke English to me when we were introduced.

"Yimi comes from where I live," Nena told them in Spanish. "It is good that he comes by here, to get to know the rancho and meet the people."

"Oh, yes," said the young men, also in Spanish, all nodding to her and seeming to ignore me.

Alejandro brought out a nickel-plated cigarette case,

passed it around, and then asked me in English, "Do you care for one?"

"No, thanks," I said.

He offered the case to Magdalena, who waved her finger in the negative. Then he sat back in his chair and lit his cigarette with the long match that was going around.

The young men fell into conversation among themselves again, and I thought they were talking about a dance they had all gone to, until I pieced together that it had been the night before, here at the rancho.

I turned to Nena. "Are there many people staying here?"

"Maybe twenty, here on a visit."

"And others come as well?"

"Oh, yes. From the other ranchos. Later there will be many people, with a great deal of food and plenty to drink. And then music. I hope you are not in a hurry."

"Not so much." I looked around. This didn't look like a bad place to sit out part of the heat of the day, as long as I didn't have to spend the whole time watching Repugno ogle Magdalena.

The young men chatted on in their light fashion. Carlos seemed to hold forth the most, while the others chipped in with their comments and oaths. The talk ran along the same vein, about parties and dances, girls that nobody wanted to dance with, and girls who kept a chin in the air and would not dance. Carlos did a comical imitation of the petulant girls, and the other fellows laughed along with him as they smoked their cigarettes and kept from looking at me. It seemed as if Carlos and Alejandro, at least, were trying to be funny for Magdalena's sake, as if she was not too delicate to hear them making fun of other girls and as if they were challenging her to be more cooperative than the others. It struck me as a boyish game, but harmless enough as we sat beneath the canopy with the breeze rippling the canvas overhead.

After we had sat there for a good ten or fifteen minutes, Nena said she wanted to introduce me to some more people. We stood up and took leave of the four young men, who all chattered polite encouragement to us to enjoy the fiesta. Rogelio then made a point of insisting that Nena not be mean with them when it came time to dance. Trying not to look at his simpering smile, I let my eyes drift from him to the other three, who were all gazing at Nena in an idle sort of way. Then, as my glance lingered on Ramón, I saw an expression cross his face. I had seen a white man look that way one time at a pretty Indian girl, with a ravenous glare that lasted but a few seconds. It was an expression that said he wanted to have that object to do whatever he wanted with it. Then Ramón was as light and breezy as the others, waving his clean, uncallused hand as Nena and I turned away.

We walked next to the place where the middle-aged men were sitting. They were a calm, pleasant-looking bunch, chatting in a matter-of-fact way. Four of the six smoked cigarettes, and of those four, three had rolled their smokes out of paper and one had rolled his out of a corn husk. I took a liking to him, in spite of his bleary eyes. He was dressed like a horseman and had a range rider's hat set back on his head. As he rose to shake hands, I noticed the big clinking rowels on his spurs, the kind that looked like they were made out of silver dollars. His name, as I caught it, was Felipe. The other men all looked like normal working folk as well, a couple of them wearing hats also, but they didn't look as if they had just blown in off the plains as he did. After Nena had introduced me around, she and I sat down and let the men fall back into their conversation. I had had my hat in my hand all this time, and now I put it on.

One of the men, who sat a little taller in his chair than the others and who had a thick head of wavy gray hair combed back on all sides, told a story about a wedding he had been to. It was at Rancho Domínguez, he said, and the party lasted all night. In the early morning, a *señora* with long white hair served a huge pot of *menudo*. After he had taken in most of his bowl of soup, he found something stuck in his throat, which he now acted out with an impressive gagging sound. He said that what he pulled out of his throat was a long white hair.

"¡Ay! ¡Hombre! ¡Qué bárbaro!" said the others.

"But the *menudo* was good, Miguel?" said Felipe, flashing a smile.

"Up until that moment. It's good for the hangover, but you lose your interest when you get a hair like that stuck in your throat."

"Oh, yes." Felipe smiled.

"Such things," said one of the other men, the only one without a mustache. "Did you get drunk last night, Felipe?"

"A madre," he answered. Then, looking at Magdalena, he said, "Excuse me."

"It's all right," she said. "It was a good party, and everyone had a good time."

The one named Miguel, who had told the story and could see I was following the Spanish all right, asked me if I liked the Mexican fiestas.

I told him I did.

"It gets good," he said. "In a little while, there will be food and beer."

I nodded.

"You don't smoke?"

"No, thanks."

He widened his eyes and smiled. "But you drink beer."

"Oh, yes."

He turned to the man without a mustache. "Someone should tell Diente Frío it's time to bring out the beer."

"¿César?" said Magdalena. "I can tell him." She rose from her chair. "Stay here, Yimi, and relax." She walked toward the kitchen, and I could see the four young men all watching her.

Another man in the group I was with, a portly man who sat with his arms across his belly and hadn't said much, spoke up. "Your story about the wedding reminded me of one I went to. This was many years ago, down by San Luis. They had the wedding in an old church in the country, and after that they had the supper and the dance. Some of the food had been sitting there all afternoon, and one dish must have gone bad, because half an hour after everyone ate, all of a sudden they all got a stomachache. Everyone, including me. It was a cramp in the stomach, with no warning, and you knew you had to drop your pants. So here were the musicians, setting down their instruments and running for the open prairie, and all the guests as well. Women in white dresses, men in their best Sunday clothes, all squatting to exonerate the abdomen, and everyone trying not to look at anyone else."

"¡Hombre!" said the others. *"¡Qué bárbaro!"*

"And where were you?" said Felipe.

"I was there, like all the others, with my pants down

around my shoes, trying to be alone and letting the others be the same way. Then it all passed over, and the festivity started again. But it was not the same."

I felt a queasy sensation run through me, followed by that better feeling that a person has when he knows that whatever the ghastly thing was, it didn't happen to him. I looked around for Magdalena, who had gone off to put a bug in someone's ear about bringing out some beer. I imagined she felt comfortable about leaving me with these men and their conversation. It seemed almost like an unspoken agreement, for as soon as she left, the round-bellied man told the story about the food poisoning.

"Here comes Diente Frío," said Felipe.

I looked around to the back part of the patio and saw a man come into the canopied area. He was a lean, dark-complexioned man, just under average height, with straight black hair, some of which stood up on the back of his head. He had large dark eyes, a bristly mustache, and a mouth that was distorted by a pair of front teeth that stuck out over his lower lip. I gathered that was how he got his nickname—Diente Frío, or Cold Tooth. The Mexicans had nicknames for everybody. The last time I saw a fellow with choppers anywhere near that prominent, his friends called him Ratoncito—Little Mouse. He was a smaller chap, and he had narrower teeth, but he could have been a cousin to this one.

"Hey, César," said Miguel. "Do you need some help with anything?"

Diente Frío raised a cigarette to his mouth and squinted as he took a puff. "No, there's not any bother," he said. "The girl said that the men were ready for some beer."

"I think she's pretty bright," said Felipe. "She saw how things were. Do you want me to help you?"

"Maybe. You could help me get out the tub and then bring some ice. I have to open a new barrel. I think you emptied the one last night."

Felipe shook his head. "Oh, no, it wasn't me. When I gave up, there were several liters in it. I think the young men finished it off."

Diente Frío cocked an eye. *"El duendecillo y sus compañeros."* The little elf and his friends.

A laugh broke out of me, but I didn't let it get too far.

Felipe stood up and nodded. "Shall we go?"

Diente Frío took a long drag on his cigarette to burn it down, then dropped the snipe and ground it out with the sole of his boot. With a jerk of the head he said, "Let's go."

As the two of them walked away, silence hung in the air for a few seconds until Miguel spoke to me again.

"So you're a friend of the dark girl?"

"Yes, I know her from the town we live in, in the north, and I knew she was here when I was passing by, so I stopped to say hello."

"Well, that's fine," he said. "But you have to be careful no one steals her. These young men are always on the lookout, ready to steal a girl from the ranchos before anyone else can get their hands on her."

"I don't think anyone's going to carry her away," I said.

"Maybe you would like to? It wouldn't be a bad idea."

I laughed. "Oh, I agree. But I'm doing some work right now. I have to go to another ranch and find about some things, and then I have to give a report to my boss."

"That's fine, but just remember, some of these young fellows are like coyotes, they steal a girl like a young pullet."

I smiled at him and nodded. He was older and wiser than I was, especially by local standards, and it wouldn't do to argue with him. I didn't see Magdalena as being in much danger, in spite of the look I had seen cross Ramón's face, and I thought she could take care of herself well enough. But I took Miguel's warning at face value and said nothing, and he turned his cheerful conversation toward his friends. I lapsed into my own thoughts then and tried to picture Rogelio the repugnant elf mounted high on a prancing stallion, with a kicking and squirming ranch girl slung across the front of his saddle. He wore a three-cornered hat and a flowing cape, and he was attended by a legion of hunchbacks, also in capes, who made up a thundering rear guard.

I left off my daydreaming when I saw the encouraging sight of Felipe and Diente Frío carrying a galvanized tub between them. As they set the tub in the shade of the canopy, I made out two glistening humps of ice. I gathered that one of the outbuildings at the rancho must be an ice-house. I hoped the beer had been kept in a cool place, so that it would not take all afternoon to cool down.

All of a sudden, I found myself taking a little too much interest in the prospect of drinking someone else's beer. Even if I was anxious for a glass of it, I didn't want to be seen, by these men or by the younger men, as a moocher. I was determined not to be one of the first in line when the beer started flowing. So I got up and walked to the edge of the canopied area, where I stood and gazed out at the area beyond the patio. I saw a graveyard of old run-down equipment—leaning wagons with missing wheels and broken axles, tipped-over plows and rusting hay rakes, an ancient steam-driven threshing machine, and a sheepherder's wagon with its rounded roof caved in. Interspersed among the implements were heaps of weathered poles, and in a couple of places a dozen or more posts had been stood up and tied together, tepee-style. I could tell that the rancho had been here for a while, and I supposed that its owners, from the earliest ones to Don Alvino, hung on to things when they were long past any use. I had known people like that. Some of them had the habit of poverty, and some of them were just optimistic, I guess.

Movement off to my right caught my attention. About thirty yards away, a rooster had flown up onto an adobe wall that rose to the height of a man's shoulders. Beyond the top of the wall, I could see calf pens sectioned off with old battered poles, and at the right end of the wall a solid wooden gate opened into the corral area. When we had been sitting with the young men, I had seen one of the older men go through the gate and then come back out a couple of minutes later, so I assumed it was a place where the men went to make water. I looked again at the array of broken-down equipment and noticed a dog chained to the wheel of a dilapidated cart. He was sitting in the shade with his nose on his paws. Then movement to my right caught my eye again, and I saw Ramón coming out of the corral and closing the gate behind him. He looked very clean and had a nonchalant air as he walked back to his friends.

I gave a moment's thought to how nice it was when a person had a wall to go behind. I recalled the story about the wedding guests, self-respecting people, all squatting in the open with no way to hide and no time to find a way. As the man had said, everyone was trying to be alone and trying to let the others be the same way. I imagined that urgency of the bowels was a great equalizer at a time like that, cutting across rich and poor, handsome and ugly, innocent and corrupt as it brought everyone to the same level. As I considered it, it seemed like a lighter version of death itself, except that it touched everyone at once. Of course, sometimes death struck that way as well, in disasters like explosions or mine cave-ins. But even in those cases, as I had heard it put, each person had to die alone. Following that line of thought, I imagined each of the wedding guests had to go through the ordeal alone, in spite of having company on any side he looked.

I wandered around the edge of the large patio or courtyard, back to the *portal* where I had come in. It was a quiet place, with a couple of benches made of planks resting on upright sections of tree trunks. A clean copper tub hung on the wall near the kitchen door, and in a dark corner stood a clay *olla* that caught my eye. I realized it was of the same design and color as the one I had seen on Doña Dolores's patio. I walked over and looked into it, only to find that it was clean and empty.

I went to the doorway and looked out at my horse standing alone at the hitch rack. He was dozing, hipshot with his head lowered, a perfect picture of unconcern. As I looked past him at the plains, I was reminded of the world beyond, where Mr. Tull was waiting for an answer and Mr. Earlywine had given someone a reason to kill him. I brushed away the image of Mr. Earlywine as I had seen him last, and I focused on Mr. Tull. I had work to do, and even if it was Sunday, I shouldn't be loafing around at a party.

A voice came up from behind me, a smooth voice in Spanish. "Yimi. Are you worried about something?"

I turned around and saw Magdalena, smiling, with a glass mug of beer in one hand and a plate of meat and beans in the other. My melancholy vanished. There was time and room enough in the world for both things. I would do some work for Mr. Tull before the day was over, and in the meantime I could enjoy some of the pleasures of a fiesta at the rancho.

Chapter Nine

The party flowed on. I have never known Mexican folk to be very concerned about clock time, but they have a good sense of timing. As the food came out of the kitchen and the beer came out of the spigot, people appeared. Some of them came from the main part of the house, some came from the sleeping quarters on the other side of the *portal,* and others, just arriving, came in from around back.

Magdalena and I sat at a table near Miguel, Felipe, and the others. I saw that the older men were drinking out of pewter mugs, which probably came from a set. The younger men, over at their table, were drinking from clear glass mugs like mine. The beer itself was all right, not very cold but not warm or bitter or sour.

As more people arrived, I noticed there was still a shortage of young single girls. I saw women with children, women with hair just turning gray, and women with white hair and sunken mouths, but I didn't see any the age of Rosa Linda and Magdalena. I asked Nena about her cousin.

"Oh, she's in the kitchen. She stays there with the other women."

"She doesn't want to come out and join the party?"

"Not just yet."

I glanced at Rogelio's table. "Then who are the young fellows going to dance with?"

"Oh, there will be a few girls when the music starts."

"When will that be?"

"A little later."

I looked around at the people sitting in their small groups—all of them calm, and some with happy expressions. Any of them, I supposed, could have things troubling them, but they were all *tranquilo,* as they would say. The only person who seemed restless was Diente Frío, who had gone back and forth between the canopied area and the place where people arrived on horseback or in buckboards. I noticed that as he walked, he looked at the ground. I had known other people who had that habit, and some of them seemed to be always on the lookout for money. By legend, at least, they were related to the fallen angel who was always looking in vain for streets paved with gold, which he would never see again. I wondered if Diente Frío was one of those people or if he was a spiritual cousin to the ones who went around with their mouths open. According to superstitions I had heard, a person like that was looking for food because when he was still in the womb, someone ate in front of his mother and did not offer her any food. Whatever the case, whether any of those beliefs were true, I imagined there were a great many people in this world who were looking for something as a matter of habit they were born to.

Magdalena had not served herself anything to eat, and I asked her if she planned to. She said yes but she wanted to be sure I was tended to first. I told her I was fine, as I had finished my plate by now. I had also noticed a pitcher of beer on the table where the older men sat, so I wasn't worried about running dry, either.

"Well, I'll go to the kitchen," she said. "I'll be back right away."

As she walked between the two rows of tables, the young men hailed her. She stopped, and they held her in conversation for a few minutes, which I tried to ignore but couldn't help glancing at. Then I turned my back on that group as I stood up and moved to the neighboring table to serve myself more beer.

Miguel gave me a knowing look, and I nodded back.

"The dark girl takes good care of you," he said.

"She's a good girl."

"Try to keep her away from those young fellows. They're not all so good, but they all give it a try."

The man who had told the story about the wedding guests said, "Whoever gets to the mill first gets his corn ground first."

"That's true," said Miguel. "When I was a boy, I would arrive there at dawn, with two buckets of boiled corn. I was not in a hurry to be first, because I liked to watch the girls bend over and roll the dough into a ball as it came out of the grinder. There were two girls, sisters, very pretty but always wrapped up in shawls, and they always had four buckets. Their family boiled corn every night and made tortillas every day. If I got there before them, I let them go first so I could watch them." He tipped his head. "But this man is right. Whoever gets there first comes out the best."

"I believe it." I nodded to both men and took my beer back to the place where I had been sitting. As I did so, I noticed that Magdalena was still talking to the young blades. Then she detached herself and went toward the kitchen.

I sat by myself for a while, sipping on my beer. Then I heard a voice in English.

"Mind if I sit down?"

I turned and saw a large man, tall and broad, with a mug of beer in his hand. "Not at all," I said. "Have a seat."

He walked around the end of the table and stood opposite me, then reached out his hand. "Name's Webb Finley."

I rose halfway from my seat to shake his hand. "I'm Jimmy Clevis."

"From around here?"

"No, just passing through. I know a couple of the people staying here, so I dropped in."

"Might as well," he said, giving a broad smile and tipping up his mug.

He seemed like a jolly sort, with a dark beard running to gray, a pair of clear eyes looking out through a pair of round spectacles, and a short-billed affair that I thought was a bicyclist's cap, though I doubted he would have ridden a bicycle all the way out to the rancho.

A Mexican woman about his own age set down a plate of meat and beans in front of him. In Spanish she asked him if he wanted tortillas, and he said yes. She asked if he wanted corn or flour tortillas, and he said flour. As she walked away, he spoke to me in English.

"The two great options in life. *Tortillas de harina, tortillas de maíz*. Doesn't it always seem that way?"

"It does." I motioned with my head in the direction of the woman. "Are you related here?"

He looked down through his glasses at the food. "Not yet. But it's one of life's options."

"Not a bad one."

"I should say not. And I've given it some thought. I'm not a passive sort, like Rip Van Winkle, you remember, who would eat white bread or brown, whichever he could get with the least trouble."

"Oh, was that in his story?"

"Yes. It's not a bad line, but he was lazy. And indiscriminate. Drank too much, but had the good fortune of having his wife die. You remember all that."

"Of course."

"But if you want to be satisfied with where you end up, you want to weigh the options, have as much to do with the outcome as you can."

"Uh-huh." I was beginning to think it was my fate to spend the day listening to the wisdom of older men.

"Gracias, Elena," he said as the woman set down a folded towel with a small stack of tortillas inside. "Help yourself," he said to me, pointing at them.

"No, thanks. I've eaten."

He went at his food in a way that convinced me he was taking his options seriously. Then he paused and said, "Just passin' through, huh?"

"Yessir."

"Well, no harm in stopping in here. These folks know how to make merry."

"That they do."

He looked past me, and I followed his gaze. Magdalena

was on her way with a plate of food. "Is that your friend?" he asked.

"Yes, it is."

He raised his eyebrows. "I didn't know there was one like that around." Then, after a frown, he added, "But you said she was just visiting."

"Yes, with her cousin."

"Cut from the same cloth?"

"Somewhat, I'd say."

"Ah, but they'll be gone anyway." He looked up and smiled as Nena set her plate on the table. *"Buenas tardes, señorita."*

They introduced themselves, and he went on to tell her, in good Spanish, that he had been having a friendly conversation with her gallant young man. He understood she was visiting here, and he hoped she enjoyed her stay. Don Alvino was a dear friend of his, for many years, and it was always a pleasure to come to the rancho. How rare it was, though, to see a flower in such bloom, and this gallant young man said there was a cousin.

Magdalena smiled and said, yes, her cousin was a niece to the widow Elena, and they were all happy to have a chance to visit.

That was the best, answered our new friend. Family was so important. The widow Elena's late husband, may he rest in peace, was a much-beloved cousin of Don Alvino. There were many fine relatives, and always more to meet.

Yes, said Nena. How nice to meet such people.

It certainly was, said the man, and he went back to his meal. After a while, he spoke to me in English. "It was a sad thing, the way Don Alvino's cousin died. He was afraid of horses, because he had been thrown from one when he was young. The horse had shied at a rope. You know the saying, if you've been bit by a snake you'll be afraid of a rope. And that's the way it was with Bernardo, only with horses. So he walked very wide of them, and he got run over by an automobile on the streets of Pueblo."

"That's too bad."

"Yes, it is. But fears run deep. There's no accounting for it." Then he turned to Nena and told her the whole story over again, in Spanish. It seemed to me that he was looking for any opportunity to sound wise, as that was his way of taking corn to the mill. He sounded quite knowledgeable about fear in particular and life in general, and he concluded his story by saying, "And in the end it was all very sad."

"Yes," said Magdalena. "How sad. And Doña Elena herself so gracious. She seems to be getting over her grief, though, thanks to relatives and friends."

Mr. Webb Finley seemed at last to be set back on his heels. He made a thoughtful job of tearing his tortilla and eating without a fork, as the Mexicans did. When he had sopped up the last of his meal, he thanked us in both languages for the pleasant company, and then he pushed himself up onto his feet and carried his plate to the kitchen.

He had an air of confidence about him as he strolled away, and I couldn't help disliking him a little. I told myself that I couldn't begrudge him for looking into the option of finding a Mexican woman for himself, as I was doing something along the same lines, though less deliberate. And even if I was jealous about another gringo being well received at the rancho, it wasn't fair for me to think of him as any more out of place than I was. On the other hand, I didn't like his know-it-all attitude, and I didn't like the way he had horned in and made himself so familiar with Magdalena. I could tolerate it more with Rogelio and Ramón than I could with him.

I had another beer as Nena ate her dinner. Time and the shadows seemed to move at a different pace, what with the canopy screening out the sun. The fiesta was pleasant, but it didn't seem to be getting anywhere now, and it didn't seem as if things were going to pick up until later in the afternoon when the music started. I went to the edge of the canopy and looked at the sun, which hung at some point between two and three in the afternoon. My sense of duty nagged at me a little stronger than the fiesta pulled at me to stay, and I decided I could probably ride to the McMasters place and get back in time for the evening festivity. I went back and told Nena what I thought.

"That should be fine, Yimi. It would be good if you could come back this way. I hope your work goes well and you don't get detained."

Don Alvino was nowhere to be seen, so I asked Nena to give him my thanks. She said she would do that but would see me to the door first. We stood up. As a matter of courtesy, I went to the next table and took leave of the men who were drinking from the pewter mugs. I explained that I had to ride to another ranch, to the south, and that I might come back later.

Felipe asked me which ranch I was going to, and I told him. He said he knew where it was, that it was in the same direction he had to go. If I wanted, he would ride along with me for a ways. I said that would be fine, my horse was out front, and I would wait for him there. I left him to finish his beer and one of his corn-husk cigarettes as I walked with Nena to the *portón.* Glancing toward the kitchen, I saw Webb Finley standing in the doorway, and I realized that the old man on the trail had been wrong when he said I'd find only Mexicans here. Then I looked back at Nena, who was much more to my liking, and we walked through the *portón* and out into the bright afternoon.

"Well, Yimi," she said. "It's too bad you have to go, but if it brings you back sooner, it's not so bad."

"I hope so. And thank you for helping me feel comfortable at the fiesta. It was all very enjoyable." I turned toward her and took her two hands in mine. "I hope I can manage to come back this way. I wouldn't want you to dance with those young men only."

"Oh, don't worry. They're just boys." She smiled. "But are you a little jealous?"

"I don't know if I have a right to be."

"Why not?"

"Well, I've never . . . you know, I am not even a *pretendiente.*"

"There's nothing to prohibit you, at least from stating your interest, if you have any."

"If I have any? What other motive would there be? It's just that I feel so stupid."

"Stupid? Why that way?"

I couldn't tell her that deep down, I was afraid—afraid that she was too much woman for me, that she knew men who were more grown up than I was, that I would make a fool of myself if I set my cap for her. "I don't know," I said. "I just feel stupid. Those are the words that come to mind."

"I don't think it's necessary to feel that way," she said. "I don't see you that way."

"Maybe it's something else, and I call it that. I think I need more courage, and it makes me feel stupid."

"Oh, that's something else," she said in a teasing tone. "But I know you have courage. I've seen it."

"In some things."

"Well, then, what are you afraid of with me?"

"I don't know. I think I'm afraid of failing."

"You have to try first. How can you fail if you don't try?"

"Maybe that's another way, by not trying."

She laughed. "Yimi, I saw you when a man was going to kill you, and you weren't afraid of anything. You carried him out on a horse. And you're afraid of a girl?"

She made a squirming motion as she smiled, but I still held both her hands, and then, as if there was nothing else in the world but the sun on my back as I stood with her outside Rancho Alegre, I was lost in a kiss with Magdalena. Even as I was lost, I had the awareness that this was a big moment, something that could not be undone or gone back on. From here on out, we would be two people who had kissed. If and when I came riding back, I would come back to that.

As we separated, she said, "I knew you would overcome your fear."

"You helped me a great deal," I said.

Then I heard hoofbeats, and I saw Felipe coming through a gate at the far end of the compound. He was riding a big sorrel that picked up its pace as it came through the gate.

I turned to Nena. *"Hasta pronto."*

"Sí, Yimi. Hasta pronto. Que te vaya bien."

Felipe and I rode south on the plains for about two miles. Neither of us spoke much until we came to the spot where he was going to turn east. At that point he made a small speech, telling me that it was a pleasure to meet me, that he wished me a good trip, and that he was at my service if I should pass this way again. I returned the courtesy with a shorter speech, gave him my hand, and reined my horse around to head south again.

I went on my way through broad, rolling country with low ridges, dotted with cedar bushes about eight to ten feet tall. From time to time I would come to a high spot, where I could pause to scan the country. The plains seemed to rise on a slow uphill grade as I went south, so that when I stopped and looked around, I could see where the landscape fell away to the north until it reached the river and then rose up again. It was a broad panorama, and I could see the general route I had taken from Cañon City to Pueblo.

A couple of miles after I took leave of Felipe, the land leveled out on a high spot where I saw a few buildings. I didn't see anyone stirring, which didn't surprise me on a Sunday afternoon. I rode within a couple hundred yards of the settlement, close enough to see a schoolhouse, a post office sign with the name of Siloam, a building that looked like a store, and a small handful of houses.

I held south, still in open country, until I came to a place where the trail forked to the right. I could see a clump of ranch buildings half a mile off, so I took that fork.

As I came close to the ranch yard, it didn't strike me as a very likely place for Raymond Bowden or any boy from town to be visiting. It was a run-down, miserable-looking outfit, with weeds growing around heaps of rubbish. A couple of dirty-looking white geese stood up in the shade of the house and started their honking sound. I rode up to within ten yards of the door and called out. I thought I heard something from inside the house, but I couldn't be sure because of the honking and hissing of the geese, so I swung down from the horse and went to rap at the front door.

I heard a hollering from within, telling me to come in. I opened the door and stepped into a dark house—dim, at least, but dark in contrast with the bright afternoon outside.

As my eyes adjusted, I saw a man sitting in a horsehair-stuffed armchair. He had a cigarette in his left hand, while his right forearm dangled from the arm of the chair and hovered over a whiskey bottle standing on the floor.

I mustered up a loud, clear voice. "I'm looking for the McMasters place."

"This is it." The man's voice had a calm, hazy tone to it.

I hesitated for a few seconds, thinking about how to frame my words. "Sorry to trouble you on a Sunday afternoon," I said, "but I was looking for another fellow, and I was told he might be here."

"Well, there's not very many people here."

"Uh-huh." I didn't need any convincing on that point. I had taken a couple of steps closer to the man, and now I could make him out. He was probably in his early forties, but his face was swollen and his eyes were dull. He hadn't shaved or even trimmed his beard in a long while, and his hair hung down scraggly over his ears. It didn't look as if he did much more than sit alone in that house and drink whiskey. I sensed that he didn't want to talk about much at all, so I tried to make it quick. "The fellow I'm looking for is a young man named Raymond Bowden," I said.

The man shook his head as he blew out a stream of smoke. "He ain't here."

"I see. Do you know him?"

"Oh, I know the little son of a bitch. But he ain't here. Never has been, unless I didn't see him."

"Huh. A man in Pueblo, name of Arthur Jeffrey, told me he thought Raymond might be staying out here."

The man shook his head again and pushed the tip of his tongue out the side of his mouth. "Nah. That little mooch wouldn't stay any place where they might expect him to do some work."

"I wonder why Mr. Jeffrey might think he was out here. Actually, he said he heard it from someone else, but even that sounds unlikely."

"No tellin'."

"Do you have any idea, then, where I might expect to find Raymond?"

"The only time I ever seen him or Jeffrey either one was in town."

"In Pueblo?"

"That's right."

"In an establishment?"

The man shifted in his seat and took another drag on his cigarette. "Yeah," he said.

I hesitated for a second. "I'm sorry for the trouble, then. I don't know why Mr. Jeffrey would have sent me out here."

"I couldn't say."

"Well, I guess I'll be on my way. Sorry for the bother."

"No bother. I wasn't doing anything anyway."

"Thanks. And thanks for telling me what you could." I looked around the room, where I could now make out small heaps of clothing, newspapers, and rags. "Is there anything I can do for you before I leave?" I didn't have any idea what I might do, but his place inside and out looked like it needed a lot done.

"I don't know what it would be," he said.

"Good enough, then, and thanks again."

I walked out into the sunlight and took what seemed like my first full breath of air in the last ten minutes. The two geese stood in the shadows and hissed at me until I climbed onto my horse and rode away.

I was more than a little put out at Mr. Jeffrey, and all I could make of it was that he had something to hide, and whatever that was, Raymond must know about it. I couldn't care about any of Mr. Jeffrey's dealings, but it looked as if I was going to have to go back and talk to him again and convince him that all I wanted to do was find Raymond.

As for Mr. McMasters, I wished I could have gotten more information from him, but I didn't think there was much to be had. And I couldn't blame him for not telling me any more than he felt like. After all, I had barged into his sitting room, where he was just trying to stay drunk and mind his own business. And I had some sympathy for people who were that far along. I had seen it in my own father, and even though there was nothing good to say about it, I knew drunks weren't happy to be that way. Sometimes they just wanted to be left alone.

I rode past Siloam again, trying to shake off the gloomy feelings from my visit with the drunk man, and trying not to let my anger at Mr. Jeffrey get the best of me, either. I looked up at the sun, which had crossed over and was reaching toward the yardarm. I imagined the people gathered at the rancho, sitting around eating and drinking and chatting. Maybe the music had begun by now. The thought cheered me.

I glanced in the direction of Pueblo. It wouldn't be that far out of my way to drop by the rancho, pay a short visit, and hit the trail again. I was probably not going to find Mr. Jeffrey until tomorrow at the earliest, and a visit at the rancho would be good for my mood.

The country looked somewhat different as I traveled back in the opposite direction, but I had no trouble finding the stand of cottonwoods and the whitewashed compound. As I came within a half mile of the front entrance, though, I was surprised to see people milling around outside. Among them was a man on horseback, who turned out to be Felipe.

As he rode up to greet me, I noted a serious look on his face.

"*¿Qué tal?*" I asked him. What's going on?

"Something bad," he said. "Someone has gotten killed."

"Really?" I felt a shock go through me. "What happened?"

He fell in beside me, and the two of us rode toward the entrance. "I was riding across the pastures," he said, "and I saw a man riding fast. It looked as if he was coming from the rancho, so I came back this way, and I found out someone had fired a shot here."

"And killed someone?"

"Yes, right outside here."

"And who got killed?"

"The young man Ramón."

I felt another tremor. I had not cared for the young man, but I hadn't wished him anything that bad.

As we rode up to the front of the rancho, I could see that the dozen people standing around were all armed men, some of them carrying pistols and some of them carrying rifles. It was only natural, I supposed, for them to turn out, even though the killer was long gone. I nodded to the ones who looked my way, and they gave me brief, stone-faced nods in return.

I dismounted and tied my horse to the hitch rack, gave a quick glance to my rifle where it rode in the scabbard, and went inside to look for Nena.

The party area, which had been calm and relaxed when I left, was in a state of turmoil. People were standing in groups, talking in loud, excited voices. I would have expected more of the women to be inside the house, until I realized that Ramón had probably been carried in and laid down. There must have been fifty people in the patio, milling and talking, so it took me a couple of minutes to find Magdalena.

"Oh, Yimi," she said. "What a terrible thing! The poor young man! You've heard what happened?"

"Only that someone shot him. I didn't hear how it happened."

"Oh, it is terrible, and Rogelio is crying because he thinks it is his fault."

"What happened, then?"

"I was not present, but everyone has told it a hundred times. Ramón and Rogelio got into an argument, and Ramón became angry at Rogelio, over something that no one will repeat. But Ramón was very angry, and he threw beer in Rogelio's face, and then he smashed his beer glass on the paving stone. After that he was ashamed and went outside, and in less time than it takes for a rooster to crow, someone fired a shot. People ran out to see what had happened, and Ramón was dead on the ground."

"What a terrible thing," I said. "It must have been someone who wasn't here at the rancho, but waiting outside."

"That's it. Felipe said he thought it was a white person, and of course people thought of you, but Felipe told them it couldn't be, because you went one way and the other man came from another."

"Huh. Does anyone know if Ramón had enemies?"

"I don't know. What everyone says is that he was quick to get angry."

"I believe it. Where is he from?"

"He is from Pueblo."

"So are a lot of people, it seems. He must have known some white people well enough for them to want to kill him."

"So it seems. They say his stepfather was white, and so are some of his friends."

"Oh, really? What's his last name?"

"Correa," she said. "I just found it out myself. He is Ramón Correa."

I gave a low whistle. "And they have him inside?"

"Yes. Don Alvino is in there with him, with some of the other *señores*. They have already sent someone for the sheriff."

"Ramón Correa, you say? And he had a white stepfather?"

"Yes. Do you think you know something?"

"I believe I do. I think the unfortunate young man in the house is one Raymond Bowden, the lost son I have been looking for."

Chapter Ten

"You should tell Don Alvino," said Magdalena. "He should know what you think."

I hesitated. "I don't know."

"Yimi, he has the right to know, and the need. The young man was killed right here at his rancho."

The ancient rules of host and guest rose before me. "I suppose you're right. I hope Don Alvino doesn't take it ill."

"Why should he, if it's the truth?"

We found Don Alvino sitting at the kitchen table with Webb Finley, Miguel, the man who had told the story about the wedding guests, and another man who looked as if he could be Don Alvino's brother.

I took off my hat, and after a brief introduction from Nena, I went on to explain in Spanish that I had been looking for a young man named Raymond, who grew up in Paloma Springs with a stepfather named Bowden and a mother named Dolores Correa. It seemed now that the young man Ramón Correa might be the one I was looking for.

Webb Finley said, in his perfect Spanish, that he knew a

few people here and there, and had heard some things, and he had no doubt that the young man here within was the selfsame Raymond.

Don Alvino turned from his friend Finley to me and asked how it came about that I was looking for the aforementioned Raymond.

I explained that I was working for an older man who wanted to find a natural son who had been lost to him.

"And the name of this older man?"

"Tull. Lawrence Tull."

Webb Finley spoke in English. "Lawrence, of virtuous father, virtuous son. Actually, it would be the other way around."

Don Alvino turned to him and asked in Spanish, "Do you know this older man, the natural father of Raymond?"

Finley, who was still wearing his bicyclist's cap and looked a bit absurd to me, raised his eyebrows and shook his head. "No. It's just a poem I'm familiar with."

Don Alvino said, still in Spanish, "Very well." Then he thanked me for my information, ending in a tone that let me know I was free to leave the kitchen. I put on my hat as I followed Nena outside.

We stood in the *portal,* apart by ourselves. "This is strange," I said. "From the time I was in Cañon City, I have felt that I was being watched and followed. It seems possible that whoever was keeping an eye on me was looking for Raymond and that I led the person here. My horse stood right outside for a couple of hours, for anyone to see. Nevertheless, whoever fired the shot at Ramón must have known who he was, to pick him out of fifty people. He must have been spying on Ramón and waiting for the chance. There are many hiding places."

"Oh, yes," she said. "Stables and lofts and storage sheds. Everyone was focused on the party. But why would someone want to kill Ramón?"

"I don't know. It could be someone who knew him and had a grudge, which could be anyone in Pueblo, or it could be someone who didn't want his natural father to find him." An image of the well-mannered Matthew Tull came to mind. "The old man has another son, who lives with him."

"Oh, then the old man has known his own blood."

"Yes, and the legitimate son might not want to share things. But I don't know if he knew about the other son. Also, I can't ignore the other possibility, that the person was from around here, someone who already knew Ramón. When I was asking around in Pueblo, a man who was supposed to be a friend of Ramón sent me off to that other ranch where Ramón would never have gone. The friend didn't want me to find him, and it must be for another reason, not just the inheritance."

"I see. So someone from either side could have done it."

"That's it."

"Was the friend in Pueblo white?"

"Yes. Wouldn't you know it? And I think I'm going to have to go back and talk to him, if I can get him to speak to me. I may have found the old man's son, but I don't have a complete report to give him. I need to see if I can get some more information from the friend."

"Well, you had better be careful. If the friend didn't want you to find Ramón, this man could be dangerous."

"Oh, yes."

"Do you think the friend did it?"

"He very well could have, but I don't think so. It was

something he could have done at any time, with less trouble. But on the other hand, it would be a good disguise to do it here." I shook my head. "Still, I don't think so. I met him, and he didn't give me that feeling."

"But he tried to get you off the track."

"Yes, but I didn't really believe him to begin with. I thought he was crooked and had something to hide. But I had to follow up on it."

"Well enough. But now you know to be careful."

"For certain."

She glanced toward the door that led outside. "When do you plan to go?"

"I think I should go this evening. I doubt that I will find him until tomorrow, but if I get there tonight, I can start early in the morning. And I might find something in the meanwhile."

"Oh, yes. You never know when the jackrabbit might jump up. And do you return here?"

"I imagine it depends on what I find. But I hope to. And you? When do you and Rosa Linda plan to leave?"

"We were going to leave tomorrow, but I think we will wait a day, to let things calm down and to give the sheriff time to ask questions of everybody."

"Well, I'll tell you. I'll try to be back here tomorrow afternoon or tomorrow evening. If I have all the information that I'm going to get, I could go with you to Colorado Espreen."

Magdalena smiled. "That would be nice. Rosa Linda would appreciate it, and I, of course, would be much indebted."

I felt my pulse quicken in a pleasurable way. "I would be delighted. I will try to be back by tomorrow afternoon.

And I hope no one sends me again, as they say in English, to chase the wild goose."

She laughed. "Don't let them do that to you. We'll expect you here."

I knew that the moment of parting had come, and with people in small groups here and there, I didn't have much of a sense of privacy. I couldn't imagine a square meter of the rancho that wasn't under surveillance at that moment, so I had to be content with brushing my lips against hers before I went on my way.

Everything looked in order as I checked my saddle and cinch. The rifle was in its scabbard, and my bedroll was tied on snug. I swung up into the saddle, touched my hat brim to Felipe as he looked my way, and put my horse into a trot and then a lope.

As I looked back, Rancho Alegre didn't seem as carefree and innocent as before, although it was the same calm set of white buildings in a grove of cottonwoods. I felt sorry for the young man Ramón, or Raymond. Even if he was corrupt in some way, it was too bad he didn't get to live a little longer and enjoy a few more of the pleasures that life had to offer. And for my part, I was sorry I didn't learn anything from him. As I had heard it put in Spanish, only the spoon knows what's ill with the pot, and he took that knowledge with him before I could get at it. It was selfish of me to think that way, I knew. He was the one who had lost everything. But I couldn't help wishing I could have gotten more out of him.

I had plenty to think about as I rode to Pueblo. Deep down, it made sense to me that Mr. Jeffrey knew the person who killed Raymond. I couldn't explain to myself why things seemed to connect that way, but they did. In a similar line of thought, which was as much gut feeling as it was logical reasoning, I suspected that Matthew Tull also had some knowledge of Raymond or even of Raymond's death. But I didn't have any sense of whether Arthur Jeffrey and Matthew Tull had a connection between them. I had no feeling on that question.

Then I had the surly Mr. Hibbard to consider. I didn't doubt that he had been following me, and he could have been doing so even at that moment. Because he was going in the same direction I was each time I saw him, beginning in Cañon City, it made the most sense that he came from Matthew Tull's side of the problem. But I couldn't imagine him firing the shot at the rancho, and I couldn't connect him with Mr. Jeffrey. It was as if each person was a spoke and there was no hub—or, now that I thought of it, Raymond was the hub, two of the others were spokes, there was no rim, and I was supposed to have a tetrahedron or a pyramid anyway. No matter how I set things up, I could tell I couldn't connect the points and was probably missing one or two as well. And judging from the success I'd had with Mr. Jeffrey the first time around, I had my doubts about how well I was going to put together the dots on my next visit. But I had to try, if I was going to make enough sense out of things to give Mr. Tull a report.

Long shadows lay across the streets of Pueblo as I rode through the center of town on my way to Mr. Jeffrey's office. The place was locked up and dark, which was normal enough on a Sunday evening. I rode around to the alley and took a look at the back door and the stable, and both of them were empty of meaning to me. Assuming that any further intelligence was going to have to wait until the morning, I found a livery stable and took care of my horse. I gave the stable man another four bits so that I would have a place to lay my bed later on. Then I went out on the street and thought about how I might kill a couple of hours.

I remembered the Silver Cloud, where I had enjoyed a couple of glasses of beer the afternoon before. I thought it would be as good a place as any, so I turned my steps in that direction. It was open, and from the doorway I saw a few patrons scattered along the bar and at the tables. I went in, taking a second look around. I didn't see anyone I recognized, though I half expected to see Kelly Kelly, Hibbard, or Long Face. I found a spot at the bar where there was a little space on either side of me, and I ordered a glass of beer.

As I took a glance to one side and another and saw what I could in the mirror as well, I gathered that the Silver Cloud lent itself to working-class men. I didn't see a necktie or white collar in the bunch, though I did see traces of coal dust, trail dust, and masonry dust in the folds of clothing, in the dents and ridges of hats, and in the creases of weathered faces.

Through my first glass and into my second, I settled into my own company. People were talking, a couple of them in loud voices, but they left me alone. And well they might. This was a drinking man's saloon, and these were Sunday drinkers—men who would drink steadily through the shank of the evening. A man at the end of the bar, sitting next to a large jar of pickled eggs, fell asleep with his head on his forearm. When the barkeep shook him, he straightened up as if he had been caught sleeping on the job. A man sitting at a table fell out of his chair, and with great difficulty he got himself back into it. Not long after that, he ordered another drink and the barkeep served him.

A young man in his early twenties took his place at the bar on my left. He had uncertain motions as he drank from his glass and set it down, and he seemed to weave as he stood there. He patted himself all over until he produced a sack of Bull Durham. Then he rolled a cigarette, made a great labor of licking and sealing it, and strained to keep his eyes open as he lit it. I took him for a stonemason's apprentice, from the dust on his clothes and the muscle in his arm. He had a short-brimmed hat set back on his head, with straight hair poking down on the sides. He looked at me and smiled, showing where decay had started a hole between his two front teeth.

"Hadderup," he said.

"You bet," I answered, without a clear notion of what he meant.

"You new here?"

"Been in here once before. Yesterday."

"Thass fine. I mean, you new in town?"

"Oh, just here for a couple of days."

He gave a broad, relaxed smile. "Not me. I live here."

"Is that right?"

"All my life."

"I see. Not a bad town, from what I've noticed."

"Not bad, but some people, they treat you like dirt."

I didn't answer.

"They think they know you."

I was sure he didn't mean me, so I nodded.

"They don't know their ass from a bass fiddle. I could tell 'em things they wished they didn't know."

"I'm sure."

He wagged his head back and forth. "But they act like they're so much better. I'll just say this. I know things and I've seen things." He squinted as he took a drag on his cigarette. "And I've done things."

"I see." Which, of course, I didn't, and I wasn't too interested in bringing out the details.

"What's your name, pal?"

"Jimmy Clevis."

"My name's Perf. Last name Moorhead."

"Mighty fine." I shook the hand that was offered. "You look like you might know some of the fellows in this town."

"A few."

"What about Arthur Jeffrey?"

Perf's face showed dislike. "He don't buy no beer."

"Mormon?"

"Far from it."

"Well, I was trying to find him."

Perf shook his head. "Can't help you there. I don't know where he keeps himself."

"Do you know any of his friends?"

"If he has any. But I'll tell ya, pal, if I knew anything about him at all, it's too much."

"Well, I can understand that," I said.

"He thinks he's a smart son of a bitch, but he's like a lot of 'em. I could tell 'em some things."

"I imagine." A movement in the mirror caught my eye, and I thought I saw the shape of Hibbard's head beneath a hat brim, but when I turned to get a better look, I saw nothing resembling him or his head.

Perf smiled. "Watchin' yer back?"

"I thought I recognized someone."

"Ah, there's no one but chumps in here. Just give 'em

one of these." He made a fist and moved it upward in a short jerk. "Jeffrey's an *A*. I could take him in a minute."

I was starting to tire of my new friend Perf, but I couldn't think of a good way to get rid of him. I looked around the barroom and saw an innocent-looking fellow, a little older than myself, sitting alone at a table. I said to Perf, "I think I do know him. I need to go see." I picked up my glass and walked away from the bar.

The man looked up as I walked toward his table. He wore a broad-brimmed, flat-crowned hat, and when he raised his head I could see a clear, open face with dark brown eyes. He had brown hair and beard, and he was about average in neatness.

"Sit down," he said.

"I thought I recognized you, but now that I'm closer, I don't think we've met." As I looked closer at him, I could see his hair and beard were running to gray.

"Only a stranger once," he said, holding out his hand as he stayed seated. "Name's Wilbur Moran."

"Mine's Jimmy Clevis." I shook hands and sat down.

"From here?"

"No, just here on an errand. And yourself?"

"Here for a while. Looking around." He pointed to a deck of cards sitting on the table near his right hand. "Do you play?"

I noted the cards, a bottle of whiskey, and a glass almost empty. "Not much."

"There's a lot in a deck of cards," he said.

"Oh, yeah."

"Drinkin' and gamblin' on the Sabbath," he went on. "Looks worse than it is."

"Oh, uh-huh."

"Are you a man of faith, Jimmy?"

I shrugged. "Somewhat, I guess."

"Well, I'm not gonna preach at you, but I've brought many a hard sinner to the Lord, and in places like this."

I nodded.

"And I've been known to tell 'em, the deck of cards is my prayer book." His eyes took on a glint and his voice went up a level as he went into his recitation. "For when I see the ace, it reminds me there is only one God. And when I see the deuce, it reminds me of the Old and New Testaments. And when I see the trey, it reminds me of the Holy Trinity—"

"Yes," I said. "I've heard that. It serves as an almanac, too, doesn't it? The four suits are for the seasons, the fifty-two cards are for the weeks, and so on?"

"That's right," he said. "There's nothin' to be feared in a deck of cards, though many shun it." He took a sip from his drink and made a motion to the barkeep. "Its best use, of course, is to help men see that sin and salvation both are part of the Lord's plan." He nodded toward the cards, then picked them up and set them in front of me. "Cut the deck, Jimmy."

I was sitting to his left, which was not the normal position for cutting the cards. As I had learned it, the player to the dealer's right was supposed to cut, just once, with his left hand, toward the dealer, no whorehouse cuts or razzle-dazzle. I didn't like cutting the cards from where I sat, so I hesitated.

"Go ahead," he said. "This is just for fun."

I cut the deck and set the upper portion near him. He snapped the top card off the remaining stack and showed the seven of clubs.

"The seven lean years, Jimmy. Do you remember that story?"

"I think I remember a couple of them. Isn't there one about Rachel and Leah, where he has to work seven years for each of them?"

"Oh, yes, there's that story, where Jacob works for Laban and then the old man plays the shell game on him with his daughters. But I'm talkin' about the one where Joseph tells the Pharaoh about the seven years of famine."

The bartender set an empty glass in front of me and moved away. Wilbur Moran tipped the bottle before I could say a word, pouring me a drink of whiskey and then one for himself.

"It's just like a young man," he said, "to remember the story about the two girls."

"Life's two options," I quipped. I was learning to defend myself in this world of wiser men.

"Indeed. Rachel and Leah, the two ways of life. But the seven lean years are worth rememberin' as well. You know, Jimmy, all the things in the Bible are what they are there, and then they're also something in the life of the everyday sinner."

He held up his drink, so I raised mine to meet it, and even though I still had beer in my other glass, I took a sip of the bitter whiskey.

"You and me both," he went on. "Sinners all. And what are the seven lean years to either of us?"

"I don't know."

"I can tell you one thing. It's a warnin', like so many things in the Bible are." He gave me a narrow look. "Have you ever heard of a judge givin' out a sentence? For seven years, perhaps?"

"That I have."

"And what sort of thing was it that the man did?"

"Oh, for a sentence like that, it's often for stealin', I guess—fellas who steal horses, or saddles, guns, jewelry, or the like."

"That's right, Jimmy. And of the numbered cards in the deck, which is the highest?"

"The ten."

"You bet. And when I see the ten, I think of the Ten Commandments that the Lord has given us. Among them it is written, 'Thou shalt not steal.' And lest a person forget that, there is the warning of the seven lean years." He took another drink. "The same goes, of course, for some of the other commandments, but you cut the seven, and we took it from there." He tipped me a wise nod and said, "Cut the deck again."

I drank down the last of my beer. "Not right now," I said.

"Oh, good enough." He gathered the cards in front of him, cracked the deck on its edge, shuffled it, cracked it a second time, and set it in front of him. Then he took it in his hand again and put it in his vest pocket.

I wondered at this last action until he rose from his seat.

"I'm goin' to visit the little house out back. Don't go away. I won't be gone but a minute."

"Sure." I didn't take it as anything personal that he didn't want to leave his deck of cards with a stranger when he was gone from the table. Furthermore, he had poured me a drink from his bottle, and I could take as long as I wanted to nip on that.

He hadn't been gone half a minute when a woman appeared on my left. I turned and saw a red-haired woman in a green dress. My first impression was that she was a hard-looking woman.

"Mind if I sit down?"

"Not at all."

"What's your name?" she asked as she drew a chair next to me and settled into it.

"Jimmy."

"Mine's Kate." She smiled, and as she did she exposed a dark hole where a couple of her side teeth were missing. I couldn't see into it very well, though it was on my side. It reminded me of the kind of pit or cavern where, in the stories, men were swallowed up and never given back to this life.

"Pleased to meet you," I said, as a line of defense.

"What are you up to tonight, Jimmy?"

"Oh, not much."

With her mouth closed, she raised her eyebrows and gave me an appraising look. "You seem like the type that knows how to have a good time."

"I've been known to, I guess."

She moved her chair closer and pushed her breast against my arm as she laid her hand on my lap. She looked at me close, with a lewd smile, and said, "I could tell."

I felt myself stir beneath her hand, but I found her resistible. Even if I hadn't developed a stronger interest and better chance with Magdalena in the last few days, I would have thought this woman was a bit too brash. I had my own phrase for a person like her. It came from the first time I heard someone read *Evangeline,* and the words "harpers hoar" fell on my ears. I had heard tell of Harpers

Ferry, so my first thought, on hearing the words without seeing them written, was that Harpers whore was some kind of a common one, that anyone might have. This woman Kate fit that idea pretty well. I didn't answer her.

She rubbed her hand on my lap as she kept her breast against me. "You don't need to be shy, you know."

"I know. It's just that I don't always warm up so fast."

She smiled, and I could see the cavern again. I thought of the Spanish word for a female person with a missing tooth. *Molacha.* It could be the name of a woman who lured sailors.

"You don't feel cold to me."

I didn't like her being that close, so I squirmed and tried to shrug her off as I said, "I'm just not warming up."

She sat back in her chair, raised her head up, moved it around, and settled down. "The night's still young," she said.

Before I could answer, a commotion broke out on my right, and I stood up to look at it and be ready if necessary. Someone had tipped over a table, spilling glasses and a bottle. One man stood looking down at another who sat on the floor, with one hand planted to hold him up.

The bartender called out from behind the bar, where he held a double-barreled shotgun straight up. "That's enough. The both of yuhs get out."

As I turned to sit down again, I thought I saw the woman Kate making some kind of a motion of drawing back from my drink.

I sat down and looked her in the eyes, which had a green hue to match her dress. "I'll tell you," I said. "I was sitting here with another fellow, as you can see, and he'll be back any minute. He's got a compulsion to talk about the Bible, so unless you want to hear a sermon on Sodom and Gomorrah . . ."

She raised her chin. "Whatever you say, Jimmy. But I don't think I miss my guess about you." She shrugged her bosom at me as she got up and left.

When her back was turned, I took advantage of the moment to study my drink. I couldn't see anything foreign in it, but I remembered all too well the headache I had when I woke up in the alley in Cañon City. I thought of tossing out the drink, and then I thought it might make an interesting experiment. After a discreet look around me, I switched it with the preacher's drink.

He came back in another minute. "What went on over there?" he asked as he sat down.

I glanced at the table that was being set up straight by the bartender and another patron. "I don't know. I didn't see it until it was over. Just someone raisin' hell, I think."

"Nothin' new." He took a full sip from his glass.

"So tell me," I said. "Are you a tent preacher?"

"Oh, not exactly, though I've done some of that."

"Mining camps and such?"

"Wherever the Lord's work takes me." He made a benevolent smile.

"Uh-huh. If I remember right, from when I first came over here, you do play cards as well as use the deck for a prayer book."

"That I do," came the quick answer.

"What do you play?"

"Oh, a little of everything. Pedro, five-card stud, Black Maria, and any of your other bunkhouse games, like cribbage or whist."

"Those are all good games."

"You bet they are. No harm in them, really. The harm's in what men do with 'em. If it's in a man's nature to throw good money after bad, it's not to be blamed on any one game. By the same token, if it's in a man's heart to cheat another, he doesn't need the euchre deck to do it."

"Now, there's a game I haven't played."

"Euchre? Oh, I've played it, too. But I used the term because that's the way some people call it when they want to make the deck seem wicked in itself. The euchre deck." He leaned back in his chair to reach into his vest pocket. As he drew out the cards and sat with his head tipped back, all of a sudden his eyes rolled upward and he went limp. His fifty-two cards scattered from his lap to the floor, and his chin came to rest on his chest. I looked at his drink glass and then all around me. Kate was nowhere to be seen, but I was convinced of one thing. If she could have gotten me to the room, she would have waited until then to slip something into my drink.

Chapter Eleven

I stayed in the Silver Cloud for about an hour longer, to make sure I knew how Mr. Wilbur Moran was going to fare. A doctor who looked like he might be Rogelio's straight-backed brother appeared, smelling of garlic sausage and beer. He took command of the scene where the bartender and some of his regular patrons had put together two tables and laid out Mr. Moran on a blanket. The doctor checked for a pulse and nodded, put a stethoscope to the man's chest, and then sniffed at the exhaled breath.

"He'll come around," said the doctor, "but he won't feel good for a while. He might need someone to help him get home." He looked around the saloon. "Did anyone save his drink? We might be able to do a test and find out what's in it."

The bartender cleared his throat. "It got spilled when we were getting him out of his chair."

I said nothing. I had already been through an interrogation by the bartender and some of the patrons, first as a suspect for tampering with the drink and then as a witness to the phantom red-haired woman, and I didn't feel I had much voice. I thought the woman was in cahoots with someone else in the place—maybe the two men who had staged the ruckus, and maybe the bartender himself, whose elbow had knocked over Wilbur Moran's glass. But I didn't sense that I was going to get anyone to look very deep, so I decided to keep to myself and get out as soon as it would look acceptable. Shortly after the doctor left, I did, too.

When I walked out onto the street, the hour was still not late. Night had fallen when I was in the Silver Cloud, but it was not yet ten o'clock, and people were out and about. I walked down the street on the left side, trying to keep my wits about me without looking suspicious of my surroundings.

A carriage came up on my right, seemed to keep pace with me for a few yards, and then pulled ahead. I came to a corner and crossed while the carriage stopped in the middle of the block ahead of me. A man in a dark coat and bowler hat got out of the coach, went into the entryway of a business, and then got back up into the carriage, which pulled away. I walked along as before, not feeling any cause for alarm, until a voice spoke to me from a recessed doorway on my left. It was a woman's voice.

"Say, fella."

I paused and looked at the dark doorway. I was sure it wasn't Kate's voice, but I couldn't see the woman very well, as she was wrapped in a long, dark, ulster-like coat.

She spoke again. "Where are you goin' in such a hurry?"

"I'm not in a hurry."

"I thought you were."

"No, I'm not."

"Do you have some place to be?"

"Not so much."

"Maybe I know a place you'd like to go, then."

The old Adam in me stirred, and I didn't think this woman was up to anything more than making her living. All the same, I remembered where I was. I said, "It sounds interesting, but I think I ought to—"

She opened her coat, and I saw the lighter color of her clothes and at least a hint of her shape. What I saw did not look bad. "It might do you some good," she said in a cozy tone.

I was about to answer when a blast ripped through the calm night. I looked up the street ahead of me, and I saw shattered glass falling on the sidewalk and street about halfway up the block—where the man had gotten down from the carriage, it seemed to me.

The girl, who had let out a small scream, asked, "What was that?"

"Some kind of an explosion," I said. "You didn't know the man in the carriage, did you?"

"What carriage?"

"The one that went by a couple of minutes ago."

"No. If I know someone in a carriage, it's not for long. What did he have to do with it?"

"He got out for a minute, went into that doorway and out, and then hightailed it. If I hadn't stopped to talk to you, I might have gone by right when it went off."

She had closed her coat and was now putting her hands in the pockets, to draw it close. "I think I"d better get out of here. I don't like these things."

"Neither do I," I said. "But take this." I handed her fifty cents, which was my loose change. Her right hand came out of the coat pocket and went back in, and I stepped aside to let her walk away. She crossed the street, turned right, and disappeared into the night.

I walked down the street, taking tentative steps in the direction of the explosion. A man appeared on the sidewalk in front of the next business down. He watched as I approached, and when I was within ten paces he spoke.

"What the hell is this?" he asked.

"It looks like someone wanted to blow something up."

"Did you see anything?"

I stopped in front of the blasted storefront and spoke to him from a few yards' distance. "I was a ways back, but I saw someone get out of a carriage, step into this doorway, then get back up into the carriage and go away."

"This is no good."

"I should say not. Do you live here?"

"I live upstairs. This is my store here." He jerked his thumb over his right shoulder.

"And what about this one?"

"It's a jeweler's. But they ought to know he puts everything in a safe."

I looked at my feet and kicked at the debris. My sole scraped on a nail head, and my toe pushed at metal fragments. I imagined there were pieces all the way out in the middle of the street. It didn't look to me as if burglary was the motive, but there I was, thinking of myself again. "This is a hell of a mess," I said. "I suppose someone should report it."

"This is no good," he said, as before.

"I'll report it," I said. "Where's a place that might have someone up at this time of night? A hotel, for instance."

"Go two blocks," he said, pointing in the direction I had

been heading. "Turn left—no, cross the street first, then turn left and go a block and a half. It's the Bristol Hotel. It's got big windows and stays lit up at night."

"I'll find it," I said.

I walked down the street, shivering now after the surprise I'd had. As the man said, this was no good. And I was damned if I was going to sleep in a stable tonight.

I went to the Bristol Hotel, but instead of saying anything about the incident a few blocks away, I took a room for the night and bought a newspaper to take to the third floor with me. Once I was inside room 323, I locked the door, propped a chair against the door handle, and crumpled up all the sheets of newspaper and scattered the wads around my bed. Then I crawled in and tried to go to sleep, all the while thinking about my pistol and rifle where I had left them in the stable.

I awoke to the first roosters crowing before dawn, but before I came awake, their crowing mixed with my dreams. It had taken me a long time to go sleep, and I had not slept well. In the jumbled world of dreams, the roosters' voices sounded like "Kelly, Kelly. My mother stuttered." Then I awoke and lay cold beneath my blankets, trying to collect my thoughts.

I heard a church bell, and when it was done I tried to remember how many times it had tolled. I thought six, and from the graying of the sky through the crack in the curtains it seemed about right. Then it sounded again, and I didn't know if it was tolling the half hour or calling people to early Mass. *Una mujer con un diente, que llama a toda la gente,* the Mexicans said. A woman with one tooth, who calls all the people.

I thought of the world outside, and it was hard to imagine that it was all the same. God-fearing people, frail old women among them, would be walking to church in the early morning, going past dark cedar and cypress trees with never a worry who might lurk there. Others, with murder in their hearts, as Wilbur Moran might say, would be sitting by lamplight or still lying beneath the covers, thinking about how to bring another person's life to an end.

Someone had thought that way about Raymond—and about Mr. Earlywine as well, now that I thought of it—and may have thought that way about me. I was convinced more than before that someone, most likely Hibbard, had tampered with my drink in Cañon City and probably for the purpose of going through my pockets. I was convinced beyond doubt that redheaded Kate had dropped something in my drink in the Silver Cloud, but I didn't have a notion as to why. Maybe it was to make it easier for someone to haul me off and dispose of me. Then, when that didn't work, they tried to get me with a shrapnel bomb. Neither was a clear attempt on my life, but they both seemed more threatening than the maneuver in Cañon City or the fight with Hibbard. Someone knew I was looking for Raymond and for information about him, and that someone wanted me off the track. As Magdalena had put it, the person could be from either side—Matthew Tull back in Monetta, which was my first guess, or Arthur Jeffrey here in Pueblo, whose hand in the game I was yet to see.

I recalled again the barrage of nails and metal fragments spraying out of the jeweler's doorway. Like the man said, it was no good.

The sun was still not up, and the crows were milling and cawing in the elm trees, when I went out into the street and made my way to the livery stable. In the gray light I saw that my horse and my gear were all as I had left them, and I felt a hurry to get saddled and packed. Then I told myself that I wouldn't be able to raise anything at Mr. Jeffrey's until eight or nine and would be wandering on the street in plain view in the meanwhile. So I laid out my bed in the straw and made myself lie down for a while, with my pistol under the covers with me.

Try as I might, I couldn't rest. I was wound up as tight as a double-bell alarm clock. As I lay there I wondered, for the thousandth time, whether I had seen Hibbard in the mirror in the Silver Cloud or whether I had projected him. Whatever the case, he wasn't the only person who had lifted a hand against me, and I was sure that whoever was behind it was higher up on the scale of things than Hibbard. It still made the most sense that the trouble was coming from Matthew Tull's side of things, but I also held on to my theory that some part of it was connected to Arthur Jeffrey's side.

The stable man was going about his morning chores now, and the horses were banging in their stalls. When I couldn't make myself lie there any longer, I rolled out of my blankets and started packing my gear again. The buildings downtown were casting deep shadows when I led the horse out into the street and climbed aboard.

I rode past Mr. Jeffrey's office, which was still closed up and dark. I went up and down a couple of blocks, turned down an alley and backtracked, and satisfied myself that no one was following me yet today. I figured someone might pick me up before the morning was over, though, especially if I was seen talking to Mr. Jeffrey again.

I rode east for a ways and then south, until I came to a

Mexican neighborhood. A man in an apron was sweeping the sidewalk in front of a grocery store. Farther down the block, another man was opening up a butcher shop. I thought of my friend Chanate, who might be opening his own shop at that moment.

When I came to a little café with wood smoke threading out of the stovepipe, I decided to have breakfast. I tied my horse to the hitching rail and went inside. A boy about ten years old stood near the cash box with a towel in his hand. He pointed at a little booth in the corner and I nodded, but before I took my seat I beckoned to him. I took out a quarter and placed it in his hand; then, pointing at my eye, I told him I needed someone to keep an eye on my horse while I had breakfast.

The café was a quiet spot in a quiet neighborhood, but it was common to have someone keep an eye on a horse, a carriage, or a wagon. And the boy was already versed in the code of honor, as I could tell by the way he kept the front door within his view.

I had a simple breakfast of eggs and beans and corn tortillas—no choice this time—followed by two cups of coffee. Everything seemed civil and reasonable in the place as I sat with no window near, wondering how many people in this small city were desperate to clamp the lid down on the pot of truth.

After paying for my meal and thanking the boy for keeping an eye on my horse, I walked out into the fresh morning. I heard the twitter of birds and the distant barking of dogs, and I thought of Raymond Bowden, or Ramón Correa, and how he would never hear the sounds of daily life again. I thought of Wilbur Moran, who might be getting a slow start on the day, through no fault of his own. I decided I would give one more day to this job and this town, and after that I would tell Mr. Tull whatever I had found out.

I led my horse down the street to a spot where someone had built up a curb and front step in front of a business that was now boarded up. Using the step to my advantage, I put my foot into the stirrup and pulled myself up onto the tall horse. Then I set off for Mr. Jeffrey's neighborhood.

I got there just as Long Face was unlocking the front door. At the sound of horse hooves, he looked my way, then pulled the key out of the door and went in. I guessed he didn't like what he saw, although I imagined he rarely liked anything. I tied my horse in front of the office, stepped onto the sidewalk, gave a short rap on the door, and walked in.

Long Face had not had time to get settled into his pose of putting his chin on his hands and his elbows on the desk, so he gave me a version of the glum stare as he stood behind his chair with his hands out of view.

"What do you need?" he asked.

"I came to see if I could talk to Mr. Jeffrey."

"I think you can see that he's not here yet."

"Do you have any idea of when he might be in?"

"When he's not in, he's out. Mr. Jeffrey keeps his own hours. I thought you understood that."

"Maybe I did." I let the silence hang for a few seconds, and I could tell he wanted me to leave, if only so he could sit down. "Tell me, though. Have you heard any news of Raymond Bowden? I went out to the ranch Mr. Jeffrey sent me to, but it was a dead end. He'd never been there."

The man showed no expression at all as he said, "I think I told you before, not too long ago, that I don't hold myself accountable for Mr. Jeffrey's personal friends or personal affairs."

"No harm in my asking, I hope."

"No good in it, either."

"Maybe you think I'm a bit too pushy," I said, still holding him there, "but I've got a job to do, and I'm just trying to do it. You might understand that, having a job yourself."

His hands moved up to the back of the chair. "You're right about one thing. I do have a job. And I try to do it when I don't get interrupted too much."

"I understand, and I won't trouble you any more at the moment." I glanced toward the desk that I took to be Mr. Jeffrey's, the dark one with the shelf of pigeonholes. The chain of two links with a key was gone from the hook. I came back to the dead stare. "So I guess I'll leave. If Mr. Jeffrey comes in, please tell him I was in. I suppose I'll come back in about an hour, if that's not too much trouble."

"Suit yourself."

I walked out and closed the door behind me, then stood on the sidewalk for a moment as I thought about the key. I imagined it belonged to the stable out back, and I wondered why a person would leave it hanging in plain view if he had something in the shed that he wanted to keep hidden. I glanced back through the window and saw that Long Face had taken a seat and had settled into his day's work of propping up his head.

As I stepped off the sidewalk and untied my horse, I wondered what I might do for the next hour. If I knew which direction Mr. Jeffrey might come from, I could keep a lookout somewhere, but I didn't even know that much. As a matter of routine, I rode around the block and turned into the alley, thinking I would decide which way to turn when I came out on the next street.

Everything was calm in the alley. The hollyhocks looked perky, and a clean long-sleeved undershirt hung on a clothesline to my left. Not far from the rubbish heap I had seen two days earlier, a striped yellow cat lay in the morning sun, licking its paw. When I came to the stable, though, one small detail seemed out of order. The chain was hanging down in two lengths, with the open padlock hooked onto the last link on the left side.

No harm, I thought, in peeking into a dusty stable. I didn't expect anything in particular, maybe some broken-down chairs or a rusted-out sheet-iron stove. When I opened the door and let in the morning sunlight, I got a surprise.

It was Mr. Jeffrey himself, lying on the dirt floor with his arms flung out and his reddish-brown hair shining in the light. His blank eyes were staring up at the cobwebs, and he had a hole in his forehead that matched the spot on Mr. Earlywine's. I bent over him, and with a delicate touch of my index finger, I lifted the right pocket on his vest. There I saw the two-link chain and the key.

I straightened up and stood back. I felt no surprise and no fear. Whoever had come after Mr. Jeffrey had come with a clear sense of purpose. Whether the person had found what he wanted in the stable, I did not know, but it was apparent that he had gotten Mr. Jeffrey to open the lock and then, after seeing inside, had followed through with a plan.

I looked down at the dead man, and if there had been anything to be surprised at, it would have been my own lack of surprise at seeing Mr. Jeffrey end up this way. As they said in Spanish, *A todo pavo le llega su hora.* To every turkey there comes his time. It was usually on the night before Christmas, according to the other saying, but it looked as if Mr. Jeffrey's time had come a little earlier that morning. When I nudged his leg with my foot, he was not stiff at all.

No sounds came from the alleyway outside, so I took another minute to glance around inside the shed. It was empty, save for a stack of dusty, warped lumber at one end and a bundle of burlap bags hanging by a piece of wire. The rafters were dark and weathered, draped in cobwebs. I wondered what someone might have been looking for in this place. It would have been something bigger than a snuffbox and smaller than a stagecoach, but beyond that, I did not have a glimmering.

I stepped backward through the doorway into the full sun, then closed the door. I had a hunch that the back door to the office was unlocked and Long Face didn't know it. Furthermore, I thought that if I knew about the back door, I might have a clearer notion of what Arthur Jeffrey did in the last few minutes before he came to grief. I could find out if the door was locked by creeping up and trying the handle, and then, when I knew what I wanted to find out, I would report the whole thing. That was my idea.

I had taken off my spurs when I got to town the night before, so I was able to take quiet steps across the back lot. I could see the door had a solid panel and no window, which could amount to either an advantage or a disadvantage. I moved forward, my steps slower now, and I paused with my hand above the doorknob. No sounds came from within, and I could picture Long Face sitting in his timeless posture, gazing at the front wall of the office.

As I turned the knob, I heard the scraping of a chair on the floorboards. Hoping to catch the man off guard if the door was unlocked, I pushed on it and flung it open when it gave. Long Face came up and around from his desk, where he was lifting a pistol out of an open drawer. I ducked as he fired wide, and then I rushed him as he cocked the gun for a second shot. I knocked him back against his chair, and the revolver went clunking onto the floor.

"Don't be a fool," I said. "I found your boss. And if you're not the one who put a bullet in him, you'd better quit acting like it."

The interrogation went on through most of the morning. Two policemen took turns going through the questions of who came in through which door on a day-to-day basis and whether the front door had been locked that morning. Long Face said his employer came and went through either door, as he wished, and that the front door had been most certainly locked that morning. Next came the question about the key to the padlock. Long Face said it always hung on the hook unless someone needed to open the shed, which he never did. From that set of information, which they did not seem satisfied with until they had backtracked several times and asked all the questions a few times, in different sequences, the police deduced that someone had either surprised Mr. Jeffrey at the back door that morning or had escorted him there so that he could go in and get the key. At some time shortly after he unlocked the shed, Mr. Jeffrey received his fatal wound.

What then, asked the police, would he have had in the stable?

Long Face said he had no idea, as he never went there and rarely stepped out the back door—except for necessity, of course.

Next came a line of questions about who knew Mr. Jeffrey, in what capacity they came by, and whether any of them might have had a reason to do him harm.

Only clients, in a business capacity, came by. And as Mr. Jeffrey had an honest business, none of his associates could have had a reason to do something like this.

And personal acquaintances?

Again, Long Face declared that he knew nothing of his employer's personal acquaintances or personal business, that Mr. Jeffrey kept things always on a professional level at the office.

The police, who had brought the conversation to this point after another circular series of questions, asked the clerk why he kept a .38 in the desk drawer and was so quick to use it.

"Because I don't like some son of a bitch to come bustin' in through the back door."

"You had the gun out before the door was open. How did you know it wasn't your boss?"

Long Face sulked, and the police pried at him with another set of questions repeated in an irregular order, until they got it out of him that Mr. Jeffrey had warned him that this fellow here—pointing at me—was nosing around and causing trouble.

The police then went to work on me, using the same methods. I let them coax it out of me that I had come to town looking for a Mr. Raymond Bowden, on behalf of a man who claimed to be his father, that I had come to this office on Saturday and had had a conversation with Mr. Jeffrey after the clerk left, and that Mr. Jeffrey had sent me on a fruitless trip to the McMasters ranch. When they had gotten all of that out of me, I volunteered my idea that the clerk must have seen his employer between Saturday afternoon and this morning, and that Mr. Jeffrey must have been worried about something.

When they asked him about it, the clerk allowed that the boss had come by where he lived and had told him to be on the lookout.

Then the police officers plied me with another hundred questions about where I had come from, who had hired me, where I had been, and who had told me what. They didn't seem very interested in the part about Paloma Springs, or even the McMasters ranch, but they perked up at the mention of Rancho Alegre.

Did I know there had been a mishap there, just last night?

Yes, I did.

Long Face was paying attention now.

And did I know who had been the victim of a shooting there?

I understood that it was the selfsame Raymond Bowden, who was called Ramón at the rancho.

"And what about the man who hired you, this Lawrence Tull? Where do you think he is?"

"I'd say he's back where I left him, in his house in Monetta, looking over his papers. Do you have information that suggests something else?"

The officer shook his head. "Just wondering."

"Well, he's an old man," I said. "I don't think he gets around very well. That's why he sent me."

"You seem to get around pretty well."

"I suppose I do. But if you want to know where I was from ten o'clock last night till half past eight this morning, I can account for every minute of it. And even if I had squeezed in a minute to get at Arthur Jeffrey, I wouldn't have come back around to try my luck with Annie Oakley here."

Long Face stiffened but said nothing.

"Well enough, Mr. Clevis. You can go now." The policeman turned to the office clerk. "I think you'd better close things up for the rest of the day, Mike, and don't stray too far from where we can find you."

I stood up and looked at the other three men in the room. I had a pretty good idea that at least one of them had heard the name Tull before, but I wasn't going to find out before I left.

Chapter Twelve

Lucky for me, Long Face Mike did not make it hard for a person to trail him. I had the impression that he assumed someone was following him—a person other than myself, someone he was afraid of—and he didn't want to see the person or to be seen looking around. When he left the office he went north for four blocks and west for three, never once turning or even looking over his shoulder. He walked in a beeline with his right hand stiff at his side and his left hand moving in normal motion. From his posture it looked as if he was carrying a knife or a pistol pointing downward, but I got close enough on a couple of occasions, by riding on cross streets, to see that it was just the way he carried his hand. I did not for a moment suspect him of murdering his boss, but I had a hunch he was urgent to tell someone what had happened. When he came to a neighborhood of well-kept houses with flower gardens and rail fences, he carried himself like a stranger to the neighborhood, and I was confident he was not going to his own digs.

He stopped in the middle of the block and rapped on an iron gate, using a small object from his pocket—something like a penknife, I imagined. Still not looking around, he rapped a second time. An older woman with tied-back gray hair came out of the house, unlatched the gate, and let him in. Less than ten minutes later, he came out and went back the way he had come, staying on the same side of the street as before and not wavering. He kept going south when he crossed the street that the office was on, and after another six blocks he turned east. From there he walked another seven blocks, and by now he was in a run-down neighborhood. When he ducked into a dark passageway between two stuccoed buildings that needed patching and paint, I figured he had returned to his own den.

I rode back to the neighborhood of the house with the iron railing. A block away, on a side street, I found a store where I was able to buy a small loaf of bread and a scrap of brick-hard cheese. The storekeeper was a short, balding man who smoked a cigar and kept a person guessing at which eye he should look into when he attempted conversation. I spoke to his left eye and told him I was interested to know who lived in a house nearby. After I described the location of the house and what it looked like, he told me it belonged to a widow lady named Mrs. Jeffrey. Mrs. Ella Jeffrey. I thanked him for his information and went out to sit on the corner, where I could gnaw on my bread and cheese as I kept an eye on the front gate of Mrs. Jeffrey's house.

After a while, when I had finished my rations and had begun to wonder how long I could sit there without feeling conspicuous, I saw a man in a suit get down from a hack that waited for him in the street. He wore one of those newer-style hats called a fedora, and he had detective written all over him. He didn't stay in the house even as long as Mike the clerk had, and he came out and got into the cab with the air of a man who had just left his laundry with the Chinaman.

Now I felt that I needed to wait a respectable amount of time, but I also had the feeling that the day was running on, and I needed to catch Mrs. Jeffrey before she decided to go somewhere. So after a long five minutes, I left my horse tied in front of the store and went on foot to the house with the iron gate.

I used the edge of a silver dollar to rap on the railing, and as the sound rang out, I felt as if all the neighbors could hear and see me. After two series of raps, the door of the house opened and a woman stepped out into a covered entryway. She stood in shadow, but I could tell it was the same gray-haired woman I had seen earlier.

"What is it?" came her voice, strained and worried.

"I'm sorry to bother you, Mrs. Jeffrey, but I'm trying to find information about a friend of your son's."

"I'll thank you not to bother me. I just found out my son has died," she said in a measured tone.

"I understand that, ma'am, and I'm sorry for your loss. I assure you I won't take up much of your time if I can ask you just a few questions."

"I've already answered some questions, and it wasn't to just anyone off the street."

"My name's Jimmy Clevis, ma'am, and I'm sorry about your son. But time is urgent right now, and I'm trying to find out a couple of things about a young man named Raymond. I'm not interested in prying into your son's affairs."

"What do you have to do with Raymond?"

"I'm working for a man who claims to be Raymond's natural father. I'm trying to get information."

"Come in through the gate," she said. "There's no use in shouting all this for the neighbors."

I reached through the railing, found the latch, and turned it. Then I walked up to within two yards of the entryway, where she stood. She didn't show any sign of moving, so I stopped and took off my hat.

She held me with her blue-gray eyes. "You can tell your employer that Raymond was killed last night. Just as my son was killed this morning. I hope you'll excuse my bitterness if I say that my son would still be alive if he had never met Raymond Bowden."

"I respect your opinion, ma'am, and I have no way of contradicting it."

"Did you already know Raymond was dead?"

"Yes, I did."

"Then what do you want?"

"I've got a hunch, as I'm sure other people do, that the same person or persons struck in both places. So I'm wondering if you could tell me of anyone who might have had it in for either or both of them."

Her face tightened and her eyes went hard as gunmetal. "I've given a name to the police, but I'm not apt to give it to any stranger who happens to come by."

I tried to give a respectful nod. "I can't blame you, ma'am." I hesitated, as if I was getting ready to leave. I was sure she wanted me to go, and I needed to try to get her to answer questions in a way that she thought would get me to leave. "Is there anything else you can tell me?"

"Not anything I can think of."

I paused. "Do you have any idea what your son might have had in the shed in back of his office?"

"No, I don't." She shook her head—too quickly, it seemed.

"I think someone was looking for something there."

"I couldn't say."

"Did Raymond take it?"

"If I don't know what was there, how do I know if Raymond took it?"

I thought I detected some resentment in her voice when the topic came around to Raymond, so I decided to work that some more. "I have a hunch that that's how Raymond got them both into trouble."

Her eyes went hard again. "Raymond was never anything *but* trouble."

"Do you think it might have been a saddle?"

"I don't know," she said again.

"I think Raymond took a saddle that Arthur had in his keeping. That's what it seems like to me." I relaxed, as if I wasn't going anywhere until I got an answer.

"Raymond made free with other people's things," she said.

I thought, *So did Arthur.* But I said, "What did he do with the saddle? I'm pretty convinced there was a saddle in that shed, and Raymond took it."

She waited for a long half-minute and then said, "I believe he left it in pawn, in some Mexican shop."

"Why did he take it to a place like that?"

"Because Raymond speaks, or rather spoke, Spanish."

"No. I mean, why did he pawn it?"

"Supposedly for safekeeping, and he could get it back. Arthur was very displeased about it."

"I can imagine. Do you have any idea of where the shop is?"

"None at all. I don't think Arthur knew, though he could have found it."

I shook my head. "It's hard to make sense of it, but I guess I'll try to find the thing." I made a motion as if I was going to put my hat on my head, and then I paused. "I just thought of something. Did your son know a man named Mr. Earlywine?"

She took a relaxed breath, as if she thought she could finally get rid of me. "Yes, he did, actually. A Mr. Milton Earlywine. Arthur used to work for him. He doesn't live here anymore." Her eyes narrowed. "Is that who you're working for?"

"No, not at all. He's just someone I came across. I have to consider everything."

"Well, I don't think he would have done any of this."

"No, ma'am, I'm sure he didn't." I gave Mrs. Jeffrey my condolences one more time, and then I left her to be alone with her sorrow. I put on my hat, and as I went through the gate I heard the door close behind me.

I went back to the store and bought a piece of jerky and a bottle of sarsaparilla. I loafed outside, with my back to Mrs. Jeffrey's place. After a few minutes I heard the click of a latch, and in the reflection of the store window, which was behind an iron grate, I saw a dark-haired person walking down the street toward my corner. In the panels of glass between the iron bars, I made out the person to be a woman, and as she crossed the street not fifty yards from me, I saw that she was dressed in the common clothes of a maid or housekeeper. She had dark hair and skin, including dark hands, and I imagined she was a mulatto or something in that way.

She took no notice of me that I could tell. She crossed the street and kept going in the same direction she had been headed. She was not a very shapely woman, and now she walked with her arms crossed and her smock pulled around in front of her, so she was not interesting to watch. In a way, that made it easier to follow her, because all I needed to think about was where she was going.

I decided to trail her from a block away, going parallel, so that if she turned on a side street, I would see her when I came to it. My plan worked all right. After six blocks she turned left, or north, and she walked on the left side of the street in the first shade of early afternoon. A block later she crossed the street, went north again for half a block, and disappeared between two buildings.

I walked straight ahead on the shady side, caught a glance of the two buildings as I walked past, and paused on the corner. Then I crossed the street, went down the block a little ways, came back to the corner, and loitered. I didn't think the hired woman would spend much time delivering the message, and for all I knew, it could have been in the form of a written note. I waited a few minutes before peeking around the corner again, and when I did, I saw her walking back in the direction she had come from. She was on the next block already, and on the shady side of the street again.

Now I had to try to figure out which door to knock on and what to ask in case it was opened by someone I didn't know. As I was pondering that idea, a tawdry-looking blond woman came out from between the two houses, turned to her left, and walked away from me on my side of the street.

She had a half-block lead on me, and I figured I needed to catch up with her after Mrs. Jeffrey's woman turned right but before she herself reached that cross street. So I stepped out, glad again I had taken my spurs off and left them with my gear.

She was a full-bodied woman, walking with purpose, so she made plenty of motion. I pushed myself and gained on her at about the rate I wanted, and even though she didn't look over her shoulder, I thought I could tell from the tilt of her head that she knew someone was coming up on her.

When I was close enough to touch her elbow if I had wanted, I spoke aloud. "Do you know Alfonso?" It was the only name I could think of at the moment that had no meaning to me.

She flinched and turned toward me, her mouth open in surprise, but she did not stop.

I saw the cavern, the dark hole that looked like a whirlpool for sailors.

"You had red hair the last time I saw you," I said. "And that wasn't so long ago."

"What do you want?" She had slowed down but not stopped, and we were getting close to the corner.

"I want to know more than I used to."

"Then go talk to someone who knows more than I do."

"I guess I could, but they wear badges, and I don't like 'em much more than you do."

That stopped her.

"What do you mean?"

"I mean, you're the little girl who slipped something

into my drink. So either you talk to me, or I talk to someone else."

She looked up and down the street and then at me. "Look," she said. "I don't have anything to say to you."

"You need to change your mind. If you're worried about someone seeing us, we can get out of the way somewhere. But if you don't want to talk, I will. It's up to you."

She gave a quick glance each way again. "All right. There's a little place on the next street, at basement level. Don't walk with me. Stay back a ways. When I go downstairs, I'll take a table and wait for you there. But I don't have a cent on me."

"That's all right. Order something, and I'll take care of it. But don't go out the back door on me."

Her eyes gave me a quick going-over. "I'll be there."

I let her go ahead, and after she had turned left, I followed. I caught sight of her just as she slowed in front of a stairway, and she went down the steps without giving me a glance. I stalled on the corner there for a minute, and then I walked down the block. When I came to the head of the stairs, which were of concrete, I turned and went down. I half expected a man with an executioner's ax at the bottom, but all I found was a pale, lean man with a fringe of hair around a cue-ball head. With a towel in his left hand, he was presiding over an empty establishment and a blend of stale odors.

He lifted his chin in the direction of a corner booth, where the woman sat with her back to me. I nodded to him and made my way across the dim room.

As I settled into the bench opposite her, she said, "I ordered something, like you said."

"That's fine."

"Do you have any cigarettes?"

"No, I don't."

She let out a sigh, flicked a glance my way, and then looked past me. "Go ahead."

"Well, I'm not sure where to begin. I suppose you know a couple of people have been killed in the last twenty-four hours."

She held her lips pressed together as she nodded.

"And I think it had something to do with what happened in the Silver Cloud last night."

She frowned and shifted her eyes to the left. A short man with bulging eyes and an enormous belly was coming our way with a crockery bowl in each hand. When he set them down in front of us, I made their contents out to be cabbage soup with some pieces of meat that looked like ham hock.

I didn't touch mine or move it closer, as she did with hers.

"I hope you don't mind," she said. "I haven't eaten yet today."

"I have. Just a little while ago." I pushed my bowl half an inch farther away.

"I don't think Pat put anything in it."

"I wouldn't have thought so. But then again, I wasn't expecting it last night, either."

"Look, I'm sorry. It wasn't my idea, and I didn't know everything that was going on."

"I hope not. All the same, I don't like someone putting something in my drink."

She made what I thought was supposed to be a coy

smile, but it looked more like a smirk. "I didn't want to do you any harm, and I really did want to get you into the room. I still don't think I missed my guess about you there." She tried her smile again.

"I don't see very much of it as being funny right now. Two men have been—"

"I know, I know," she cut in, frowning as she motioned toward the proprietor.

I stared at her and spoke in a lower voice. "Who put you up to it, then?"

She looked at her soup and got her spoon under a chip of meat. "I don't think I can tell you that."

I looked around at the dark walls. "What did we come here for?"

"To talk."

"Well, then, talk. Who put you up to it?"

"Ask me something else."

"Did you know the two young men who died?"

"Yes."

"And the mother of one of them?"

"Yes. Her, too."

"And the father of the other?"

She shook her head. "Don't know anything there."

"Or the father's other son?"

She moved her head back and forth. "Can't say."

"Well, let me prime the pump, though I don't think I'll be telling you anything you haven't already heard."

"You never know."

"I guess not. Well, to begin with, I took a job with a fellow, an older man, who claims to be Raymond's father. The job took me to Paloma Springs, then here to Pueblo, then to a place in the country called Rancho Alegre. And everywhere I go, there seems to be a connection I can't figure out."

"I can imagine."

"I suppose you can. The way I see it, someone's got a hell of a big secret, and someone else has been trying to make money off of it."

"That's pretty close."

"And whoever has been making money has been put out of business."

"Uh-huh."

"Do you know a fellow named Earlywine?"

"Not directly. I just know who he is."

"Or was. He ended up with a hole in his forehead, just like Arthur."

She shuddered. "I didn't know anyone was going to do that to Arthur."

"So I need to find out what the connection is, before someone else—notably myself—gets hurt."

She finished what she was chewing and then said, "I don't know how much I can tell you without having something happen to me."

"Well, without mentioning names, let me ask some questions about 'him.' "

"I just don't—"

"Look. Consider yourself the golden goose here. I'm not going to tell anyone I talked to you. Why should I?" I nudged my soup bowl toward her. "Here. I really did have something to eat earlier. Have as much of this as you care for."

She didn't say anything, and I had the feeling I was going to have to start all over again. "So," I said, "is your name Kate?"

"When I want it to be."

"Good enough, then, Kate. Let me ask some questions about this other person, who doesn't have a name."

She shrugged.

"Did he know Arthur?"

"Yes."

"Did he know Raymond?"

"He knew *about* Raymond more than he actually knew him. I think he had probably met Raymond, but I don't know."

"I see. And how did he get to know Arthur?"

"Actually, through Raymond."

"How so?"

"He learned about Raymond somehow, and he wanted to get to know more and keep track of him, so he made friends with Arthur. I think he might even have helped him out in business."

"Helped Arthur."

"Yes."

"How long ago was this?"

"I don't know. Six or seven years, maybe more."

"And then what happened?"

She shrugged and started fishing around in the second bowl of soup.

"Something else happened," I said, "or there wouldn't be a secret."

Kate let out a sigh. "This person, this 'him,' took an interest in Arthur's mother. She was an attractive lady then—she still is, but she was younger then, and still trying to hang on to her beauty."

"And I suppose she was flattered by this younger man's attentions?"

"Whew. It was more than attention. He was absolutely obsessed with her. And, yes, she was flattered, but she did her best to hold him off for quite a while."

"But then she gave in, you might say."

"Yes."

"And how long did this go on?"

"Maybe four years. He came to town pretty often."

"But then it didn't last."

"No. And at about that time, Arthur found out, and there were some very hard feelings."

"Is that what ended it?"

"I don't know."

"Do you think he has another love interest now, maybe someone closer to his own age?"

"I have no idea. It would be a natural thing to happen."

"And Mr. Earlywine, or Arthur, or anyone else, might have used this bit of earlier history, in light of this new interest?"

"That I don't know."

"But there was certainly some earlier history to be used."

"Yes, there was."

"Well, that's too bad. Mrs. Jeffrey doesn't seem to have done too well by it."

"She lost her good looks. Just let herself go after that."

"I didn't mean that, but I suppose that's evident, too. What I meant was that she lost a son."

"Well, yes."

"But she seems inclined to blame it on Raymond more than anything else."

"Oh, yes. Arthur knew Raymond before any of this other business happened."

"I think I had that in place, as far as time goes. Was Raymond as bad an influence as Mrs. Jeffrey makes it out? From the impression I got from the neighbors in Paloma Springs, I thought Arthur might have been the city mouse and Raymond the country mouse."

"Mrs. Jeffrey would blame someone else no matter what, because her little boy wouldn't do anything wrong. But the truth is, Arthur had a strong attraction toward Raymond, and Raymond was rather cruel about it. He would lead him on and then shut him out. He made a fool of Arthur, and Mrs. Jeffrey hated him for it."

"Not unlike the way Arthur wanted to spite his ex-friend."

"You mean 'him'? I suppose so."

I thought we were nearing the end of our conversation, so I threw out a question that I wouldn't have asked earlier if I had thought of it. "So who did you know first, Arthur or him?"

"Arthur. Until I got to know him—Arthur, that is—better."

"And that's how you got to know what's-his-name, through Arthur?"

"I never said I knew him."

"Oh. I see. But you've remained friends with Mrs. Jeffrey, in spite of other things?"

"At a distance, but yes."

"I feel sorry for her at a time like this. She has to have some regrets as well as resentments."

"I'm sure."

"I even feel sorry for Mike the clerk."

"Oh, Mike. I just see him as an old punk. But I guess

you're right. He probably didn't have any other friends but Arthur."

When Kate was gone, I paid my bill with the proprietor. As I handed him a dollar, I asked, "Does it ever get busy in here?"

"No," he said. "You're the only person that's been in here for the last hour."

"Yeah," I said. "And I was hoping to meet my sister here." As he went to give me the fifty cents in change, I waved to him to keep it. Then I climbed up the stairs and into the bright day.

I stood there on the sidewalk for a few minutes, breathing the fresh air and looking around. It was a hospitable summer afternoon, I thought, with blue sky and warm sun. A slight breeze riffled the leaves on an elm tree across the street, and I caught the aroma of baking bread. I imagined that in many of the houses in this town, women were kneading or rolling out dough for bread or pies, while in businesses and shops, men were thinking about the pleasures of hearth and home.

Elsewhere, I could imagine women afraid to speak or afraid of what they had said, just as I could picture men brooding about how their women might have spoken to someone during the day.

I looked at the benevolent sky again. Somewhere in this small city, I thought, in some pawnshop or saddle shop, there was a saddle that told a story. If I could find it, it would help Mr. Earlywine and others speak from beyond the grave—or, if not speak, at least point a finger.

Chapter Thirteen

Although Sister Kate, as I thought to call her, had avoided stating a name, I had a pretty good idea it was Matthew Tull—or information about him—that I was after. The only other person who rose to the level of a possible suspect was Hibbard, and I couldn't imagine any motives for him to be putting holes in men's foreheads, unless he was doing it for Tull. Furthermore, I could not picture him as Mrs. Jeffrey's paramour. Matthew Tull, on the other hand, fit in every way. He had two strong motives in wanting to protect his inheritance and in wanting to keep a secret from going any farther, and both of those motives could have been operating when he—or Hibbard, to keep the options open—pulled the trigger on Ramón. Raymond in town, Ramón at the rancho, he could have loomed as a possible blackmailer. It seemed as if he had no qualms about being an opportunist. But I couldn't see where he had any secrets of his own to protect. With Matthew it made me think of the phrase "like father, like son." It was too bad people got killed over other people's secrets, especially when it didn't seem to be that much to be ashamed of, but in the case of Mr. Earlywine and Arthur Jeffrey, they chose to try to take advantage of someone else's privacy. That was their mistake.

I tried to shake my head clear of some of the murky business so I could concentrate on what I needed to do. I had to give a report to Mr. Tull, and since my conclusions were going to come close to home with him, I thought I had better get some physical proof if I could.

Finding my horse where I left him and seeing that everything was still in order, I set out for the Mexican part of town I had found earlier. I figured it was still siesta time, between one and three, when many people closed up shop for the midday meal and whatever else they did. But I thought I would get started looking for places at least.

When I asked around, no one seemed to know of any pawnshops in this part of town, but they were able to tell me of a couple of places that bought and sold all things for horses. Following directions, I found a shop that had a multitude of saddles. I peeked in through a large glass window, which was covered by an iron railing, or *reja,* as they called it. The front entrance also had another door of ironwork, and it was closed. I noted again the name of the place, Rancho del Norte, and went on my way.

On a side street I found a second place that had been mentioned, a dark little shop, and its door was open. The storefront had old wooden steps and a coarse-grained door casing, all smooth and darkened by oil. A wizened little man with a long gray mustache invited me in and put himself at my service. I told him I was looking for saddles and other things.

He showed me two saddles, both of them old and dark,

with tight layers of leather that looked as if they hadn't been disturbed since the days of Maximilian.

"These are rather old," I said in Spanish.

"Oh, yes. Very good ones."

"Have you had them for long?"

"One year, maybe two. I take good care of them."

"I see. You have very good merchandise." I looked around.

"Something else? A *sudadero?*" He showed me a saddle blanket that folded twice, so that it had three layers. Easy to change when one side got too sweaty, he explained.

I looked at a collection of bit chains he had hanging on a piece of wire tied to two nails. "These are good," I said. "Some of the cowboys call them slobber chains."

The man laughed. "Oh, yes. So the horse doesn't chew the reins."

"They also make the reins longer. They would be useful to me. My horse has a long neck."

"Of course. Do you care for them?"

"How much are they worth?"

"Twenty-five cents."

"Each?"

"No, for the pair."

"Very well." I paid him for the chains, and he dropped them in a limp little pile into my palm. I went out into the bright afternoon and put them in my saddlebag.

When I got back to Rancho del Norte, a man who looked as if he had made the best out of a two-hour mealtime was unlocking the *reja* with a big jingle of keys. I swung down from my horse, tied him to the rail, and went into the shop.

"What do you look for?" asked the man, setting his keys somewhere underneath the counter.

"Oh, a saddle, perhaps."

"Very well. I have many saddles."

"So I see."

He stepped forward and made a sweeping motion with his arm. "Do you care to see them?"

"I think so." I paused at a row of about six. "Are these all yours to sell?"

"Oh, yes. They are all mine. I can sell any one or all of them to you. How many do you want?"

"Just one, at the most." I had to think for a minute. Raymond was thought to have pawned the saddle, but if he was unable to do that, he may have sold it outright and then said he pawned it.

"A new one, perhaps, or a used one?"

"Probably a used one, but I need to look very carefully."

"At your service. Go ahead."

I looked at one saddle after another, beginning with the used ones. Several of them looked like the two I had seen in the other shop—old and tight. Some of them had rosettes snugged deep against the leather, with ancient crevices of dust along the fringes where the cloth didn't reach. Some had skirts that were curled and warped, and some had fenders that were worn and cracked. One had mismatched stirrups.

I came to a row of new ones and looked at them. They had a sameness to them, all rigid and shiny, with new latigos and strings, and horn wraps that had never known the scuff of a rope.

I went back to the used saddles, still looking for one that showed signs of having been taken apart or worked on. According to Mr. Earlywine, there was a set of initials stamped somewhere out of sight, and I was assuming that someone would have taken the saddle apart to do the engraving, and someone else might have taken it apart to try to find the initials. I found one saddle that had had the stirrup leathers replaced, and one that had new strings. I remembered what Mr. Earlywine had said—they can change the stirrups, the conchos, the rosettes, or the strings, but they can't change something they don't know about.

I looked for a while at the one that had new strings. I could imagine Arthur and maybe Raymond not being able to get the old strings untied and then cutting them to get at the layers. Then they would have to put it back together. I looked at the strings where they were snugged against the rosettes in the tight knots that saddlemakers use, putting a slit in one string, passing the other through, twisting it, and then doing the same again. These strings weren't put in by an amateur. But it was the only one that looked as if it had been taken apart.

Moving on, I looked over the rest of the saddles. Some of them were the old Mexican style with a horn as big as a dinner plate, and some were of rawhide or rough-out leather. Most, though, were made of tooled and polished leather, with skirts and fenders and capped horns.

I came back to the one with the new strings. Anyone who had cut the old strings could have had someone put in the new ones. I turned to the shopkeeper, who was standing by. "Did you change the strings on this one?"

"Did I change what?"

"The strings." As I said it in Spanish, *las correas,* I realized I was saying Ramón's last name.

"No, it came to me that way."

"Oh, really? Do you remember when you bought it?"

"Yes, it was last fall. When we had the first snow."

My spirits sank. Now I had to find another likely specimen. "What is your most recent one?" I asked.

"These," he said, pointing to a row of shiny new saddles, the ones I had already looked over.

"Oh, yes. Do you have any used ones that you bought recently?"

"What does it matter? They keep better in here than they do outside or in a barn. I clean them all with oil and a rag."

"I can see that. They all look very clean and well cared for."

He nodded, as if I had said something reasonable. "That one there is in very good condition," he said, pointing at the one with new strings. "Very comfortable, from being used, but clean and well-repaired."

"Yes, indeed. And how much is a saddle like this one worth?"

"I can sell it to you for some twenty-five dollars."

I almost choked. I could buy a new one for that price, or pretty close. I looked at the saddle but said nothing.

"Do you wish to buy it?"

"I don't think so. The saddle I am looking for is something like this, but I don't think this is the one."

"A saddle such as this one keeps its value very well."

"Yes, but to tell you something in confidence, I am looking for a saddle that someone took to a shop not very long ago, so I don't think this one is it."

The man raised his eyebrows. "If you are looking for something that is lost, you should be able to recognize it when you see it."

"I did not lose it. Someone else did, and I was given to

understand that the people who took it might then have sold it."

He raised one side of his mustache. "Please do not think I do business of that kind."

"I do not think such a thing."

"Very well. But it seems as if you do not really wish to buy a saddle. Just to ask questions."

"I am willing to buy a saddle, if I think it is the one I am looking for. But I cannot buy a pile of them."

He stood glaring at me as if I were the one who had been making off with other people's property. "So you are looking for a saddle you have not seen and do not know, but you would like to have it in your possession?"

"Yes," I said in as cheerful a tone as I could. "I have great interest in it and would be willing to buy it if I am convinced it's the one I am looking for." I realized it would be hard for me to buy any saddle, even a moldy old thing with a broken tree, for less than twenty-five dollars at this point.

"Look around," he said. "But if you don't know which one it is, or what it looks like—"

"What I would like," I said, "is to see the saddle you have acquired most recently."

He made a slow nod, as if he was conceding something in argument. "Very well. Come this way." He led me to the middle of his store and pointed out a Texas-style double-rigged outfit with slick forks, taps on the stirrups, and about ten sets of strings. "Is this your saddle?"

I shrugged. "I don't know. When did you take it in?"

"On Saturday. And it is a much better saddle than the one you were looking at a little while ago."

Saturday. From what I understood, Ramón would have

gotten to the rancho by then. I shook my head. "I don't think this is the one." I looked around the shop at what now looked like a sea of saddles. "I don't think this is it, and I don't think the other one is, either. The one I hope to find would have been sold last week or the week before."

The man stood with his arms crossed high on his stomach, a studied look on his face. I thought he could see himself closing in on a sale. "I took in two saddles during that time," he said, "and I sold one."

"Ah, very good. And where is the other?"

"Over here." He led me to the one with the new strings and waved his hand in its direction.

"Excuse me," I said, "but I believe you told me you bought that one during the first snowfall last year."

"No, not that one. The one next to it."

I let my gaze settle on the one he now pointed at. It looked no different from a dozen others—double-rigged, square skirts, slick forks, and plain, open stirrups. It had roses and curlicues stamped all around the borders.

"Do you know a young man named Ramón?" I asked.

"I know various young men Ramón."

"Did some Ramón bring in this saddle?"

"I did not ask the name," he said, with something of the same indignant tone he had used when he said he didn't do business of that kind.

I gave the object a closer look, but there wasn't a thing about it that called my attention. Everything seemed normal, in order, undisturbed. I ran my fingers down the cantle, across the seat, and up onto the cap of the horn. I could see the stitching all the way around the rim.

"This is covered in leather," I said, tapping the crown.

"Yes, sir. It is."

"What is it made of inside?"

"The old ones were wood, but these are of iron. Like those." He pointed at a cluster of bare saddle horns he had hanging on the wall. They hung on a wire like a string of fish, but they looked like turtles made of lead.

I tapped again on the one in front of me. "Aren't some of them made of brass?"

"Oh, yes. But iron is more common."

I picked up a stirrup, looked at the leather underneath the fender, and let it down. "A young man sold this in the last two weeks?"

"In that time I acquired it, yes."

"Very well. And how much is it worth?"

"It is a better saddle than the other one there, but I could let you have it for the same price."

"And that price?"

"Twenty-five dollars, like before."

I stood back. "I don't know." I gave the man a direct look, hoping he would see I was talking straight. "The saddle I am looking for is supposed to have some letters, the initials of someone's name, engraved in a hidden place."

"If it is hidden, who can find it like this?"

"Exactly. It might be on a layer of leather underneath, or it might be in the metal of the saddle horn."

"If it is there at all."

"Yes. And, of course, I do not want to buy the wrong saddle."

"That is for you to decide."

"What would you think," I said, "if I just cut the thread around the crown here? How much would that be worth? Then, if it was the one, I would buy the whole saddle."

He shook his head. "You have many ideas. If the letters

are there, it tells you it is the saddle you are looking for. If they are not there, it tells you nothing. Then you will want to cut the strings and take apart all the layers." He crossed his arms on his stomach again. "If you want it, buy it. Then it is yours to do with what you want."

"And the other one you bought during that time?"

"It has been sold."

"I know. But what kind of a person brought it in?"

"That does not interest you very much. But it was not your Ramón, I can tell you that."

I looked at the saddle, still trying to get some kind of a hunch. Twenty-five dollars was a large part of what I had left, and I couldn't buy these things all day long, just for the pleasure of cutting them apart. I had to accept the possibility that I might not find out anything for certain, and if that was the case, that was how I was going to have to make my report. Meanwhile, this was the best bet I had, and I needed to get back to the rancho. I had a good reason to be there and another good reason not to be traveling after dark.

"Very well," I said. "I'll give it a try." I dug out a twenty-dollar gold piece and another for five, and I handed the coins to him.

He tilted his head forward, in a kind of a bow, and he said, "It is yours."

I pulled the saddle and its stand out and away from the others. Then I took out my pocketknife, opened the blade, and started cutting the stitches around the leather cap of the saddle horn. When I had them all cut, I peeled back the leather.

The metal beneath was brass, about two inches across and not perfectly smooth. At first I thought I saw the letters *LW,* but then I realized I was reading them upside down. I shifted position so that I was standing side by side with the saddle, and with my right thumb holding back the leather, I cupped my left hand to take away some of the glare of the daylight. Then I read the letters, clearly etched, as *MT*.

I looked at the shop owner, who was craning his neck but keeping an indifferent expression on his face.

"I think I found what I was looking for."

"How good. For you."

I stood back and left the saddle on its stand. "How much would it cost me to have it sewn up again?"

"What do you mean?"

"Well, to sew it around the edge." I pointed and made a small circular motion with my finger.

"Always with ideas. I do not do that kind of work. You will have to take it to someone who does it."

I looked at the cut stitching and back at him. "Can you recommend someone? Does the little old man around the corner do work like that?"

"I don't know. You'll have to ask him. But that's yours, and you can take it with you."

He held the door open as I carried out the thing I had paid for. It was hard for me to think of it as mine, but it was the object I was looking for, and I had it in my possession. What I needed now was to get it stitched together and decide when I could come by again to pick it up.

I had to admit I was pleased with myself. I had found what I was after, and I had gotten it without much trouble. Except for that one moment when Long Face Mike pulled out his .38, I had managed to stay away from back doors, go in the front, and pay my way fair and square. I hadn't tried to chisel the old man a nickel on the price of the slobber chains, and I supposed he would be happy to see me again.

Although I had said "around the corner," the old man's shop was two blocks down and then a block and a half to the right as the street sloped downhill. This part of town didn't have sidewalks but rather hard-packed dirt paths, so I tried to keep an eye out as I carried the saddle in front of me with both hands.

I turned the corner and adjusted my grip for going downhill. As I came to the alleyway, a figure stepped out. I recognized the broad-brimmed hat and the close-cropped head it shaded, then the thick neck and bulky shoulders. It gave me a jolt of worry, but I was not surprised to run into Hibbard again.

I tried to walk around him, but he sidestepped in front of me. I stopped at the edge of the street, thinking that if I just stood there in the open, I would have the general protection of being in the public eye.

"I'll thank you to get out of my way," I said.

"You might save your thanks until they're needed. And as far as that's concerned, you're in my way."

"I hardly think so. You've been trailing me for days, and I don't like it."

He made an expression between a grimace and a smile, showing the picket fence. "You don't have to like it. What do you think you're doing here, anyway?"

"What does it look like? I'm looking for a place to get a saddle repaired."

"Well, if you didn't have your hands full, I'd think you were lookin' for a place to get drunk, maybe put your nose between a woman's legs."

"Even if I was, what's it to you?"

"Not much, as long as you stick to your little brown-skinned greasers. But you ought to watch yourself around the others."

"So I've learned."

"Maybe you haven't learned enough."

"What do you mean by that?" I told myself to be careful. It looked as if he was bringing something on, and I remembered to keep an eye out for the left hand.

"I don't like someone sneakin' around with my girl."

"Your girl?" It seemed preposterous that he would call her that, and I imagined he was using it just to start a fight. I figured my best bet right now was to stand there in the street and hope someone came along. I had already decided, on the basis of the other times we crossed paths, that he wasn't going to do me in, or he would have done it earlier. So I thought I could try to string things out. "Ah, go on," I said. "If she's your girl, you ought to get her into some other line of work, like pumping the treadle on a sewing machine."

"You're pretty smart for a little drunk. But I'm telling you, I don't want you around her, and I don't like you buying jewelry for her."

"What jewelry?"

He held his left hand up and out at the level of his hat brim, and he held hanging from his fingertips the pair of bit chains I had just bought. They glinted in the sun.

"Hey, what the hell—?"

He opened his fingers and let the chains drop, and as I stretched to look at them, he stepped forward and came around with his right hand. Something rapped me behind my left ear. I saw a shower of sparks, and then my lights went out.

* * *

When I came to, I realized someone was crouched by me giving me shade. The person spoke in Spanish.

"Are you all right, young man?"

I shook my head and looked at him. It was the old man from the first shop I went into. "I think so," I said. "Someone gave me a good one."

"Did they take your money? They didn't take your chains."

I sat up and looked around. My hat was on the ground, about three feet from the bit chains. "No," I said. "He didn't want my money. He took my saddle."

Chapter Fourteen

All the way back to Rancho Alegre, I wondered how I was going to give my report to Mr. Tull. I could tell him what I knew for sure, which began and ended with Raymond, or I could tell him my theories and assure him I did see something resembling proof. If Matthew had left his father's house, which I imagined he had done, he would be back under the same roof by the time I returned, so I would have to be prepared to talk to the father with the son somewhere near at hand.

That was the worst of it, I thought—Matthew on the loose. Up until I found the saddle, he had no reason to dispatch me or have Hibbard do it. To the contrary, I was useful to them, as it now seemed. I led them to Raymond, however unintentionally, and I found the saddle. Now, instead of being their bird dog, I represented a danger. I had seen the initials on the saddle horn, and I was expected to make a report to Mr. Tull, senior.

According to Mrs. Jeffrey, she had given the police a name. But until someone sighted Matthew, no one would know to look for him in Pueblo, much less where. I suspected he was holed up somewhere in town, but it was only a feeling. Although I had no proof, I thought he had been in the carriage the night the bomb went off in the jeweler's doorway. I also imagined he was looking over the trophy that Hibbard had brought to him, and if they hadn't had that distraction, one or both of them would have been on my trail already.

Maybe they were, but I trusted I had a good lead on them. I reached forward and patted the long neck of my horse. I told him he was a good boy and there would be a bait of grub for him when we got to the rancho.

I let him out on a lope, and the landscape flowed by. I had been on this trail a couple of times already, so I had a general idea of what to expect. I kept a sharp eye out when we went though the big draws, and I skirted a couple of places that I thought were possible hiding spots. By and by I came out on higher ground, and I breathed easier. I turned off the main trail at about the spot where I had seen the old man repairing his outfit, and I headed across country to the stand of cottonwoods and the patches of white buildings I could see between the tree trunks.

As I rode toward the front of the rancho, it looked quiet and sober in the late-afternoon sunlight. Off to the far end where the corrals were, I saw dust rising, but no people or animals were in view anywhere. I assumed most of the guests had gone home after the fiesta, and I imagined those who were still around would be feeling a little subdued and keeping close to the house. Still, I felt happy myself at the prospect of seeing Magdalena.

Diente Frío met me at the door, and after a few words he let me in and went to find the *muchacha,* as he called her. I stood alone in the entryway with my hat in my hand for about five minutes, and then, with a rush of breath, Nena appeared. She was wearing a dark blue cotton dress and solid red earrings, and it looked as if she hadn't been too long out of the bathtub. She had a cool, calm air about her, but not too serious for a smile.

"Yimi, how good to see you. You had a safe trip?"

"Yes, thanks to God. One never knows."

"That's true. Did you find out anything in town?"

"A few things. Has there been any news?"

Her brows tightened. "There came news that a friend of Ramón's got killed in Pueblo. The large American says he knew him."

"Oh, *el señor* Webb Finley. Is he still here?"

"Yes, he leaves tomorrow, to accompany Doña Elena to Pueblo."

"I suppose he knows everything except who fired the shots. Maybe he knows that, too."

"He seems to know many people. He says he knows of Ramón's natural father and he knows who the other son is."

"Indeed. He knows a great deal, doesn't he?"

"He gives that impression."

I touched the side of my nose. "Do you find him somewhat snoopy?"

She laughed, as people sometimes did when I used the word *metiche*. "I suppose that's how he comes to know so many things," she said.

"So he knows young Mr. Tull."

"Apparently."

I looked at her. "I didn't think of this before, but you might know him, too."

"How?"

"He lives most of the time in his father's house, there in Monetta, on the other side of the river."

"Oh, it could be. I don't know a great many people on that side. What is he like?"

I tried to envision him. "He has blond hair and blue eyes, and a blond mustache. A little taller than I am, always well dressed, in good physical condition. Well mannered, smiles a lot, and his eye goes everywhere."

"And his name?"

I looked around and did not say it very loud. "Matthew Tull."

Magdalena frowned. "I'm not sure of the name. I have seen a man like that, a few times. He comes to our side to look for girls."

"That could very well be him." I hesitated on my next question. "Have you ever talked to him?"

"No. He looks for girls, but I don't know if any of them talk to him. They call him 'Velvet Coat.' "

I could picture him, with a vest as well, and a watch chain. "Well, he may be around here—in Pueblo, that is. I think that either he or a brute who works for him is responsible for the death of Ramón, his friend in town, and the fat man who died before I left Monetta."

Magdalena took in a quick breath of air. "Yimi! He sounds like a dangerous man. And you are working for his father."

"Precisely. So we have to be on the lookout. Especially myself. I have learned things that do not favor him." I paused to think back on something else I had told her. "By the way, he has a hard fellow working for him."

"A brute, you said."

"Yes. He wears a broad black hat, and he has very short hair, as if he shaves his head. And his teeth, they are like a fence of white boards with spaces in between."

She laughed. "Oh, like a piano."

I laughed with her. "Yes, like the keys on a piano. Have you seen anyone like that?"

"Maybe with teeth that way, but not with a shaved head."

"Not here, or in Florence, or back in Monetta?"

She shook her head. "Not that I noticed."

"Well, he may have seen us together. We need to be on the lookout for him and Velvet Coat, the two of them."

"Very well. I don't think they will come to the rancho. Not inside." She put her hand on my arm. "Do you stay here tonight, Yimi?"

"If it's all right. My horse is still outside, of course."

"I'm sure it is fine. I will ask César to put him away."

"I can tend to my horse, as long as I know I am not—"

"It's fine. I will speak to César."

She left me in the *portal* as she went in search of Diente Frío. In a little while, she returned with him trailing behind at a shuffle, smoking a cigarette and looking at the paving stones in the courtyard.

"He will show you," she said.

I put on my hat and followed Diente Frío out through the *portón*. He stood kicking the dirt as I untied my horse, and then he led me around to the corrals. He pointed out a pen that had a couple of other horses in it, so I stripped my horse and turned him in with the others. He went right to the hayrack and started eating. I picked up my gear from the ground and asked where I should put it.

Anywhere, said Diente Frío. No one bothered anything here at the rancho.

Was there a bunkhouse or something, I asked, where the workers slept?

Better to not put anything there. The young boys got into everything, looking for hidden candy. Better to go to the rooms for the invited people.

Where was that?

He led me around the back way and across the courtyard to the set of rooms that ran opposite from the kitchen on the other side of the entryway. It was a long walk, as I carried all my gear together and had my rifle scabbard banging on my legs the whole way.

My guide stopped at the third room, which had an ancient sagging door of thick lumber. He lifted the door and opened it, and I found myself inside a dim room of about twelve feet by twelve. The walls had been plastered and whitewashed at some time in the past, but now they looked smoky and cobwebby. Straight across from me, a small cast-iron stove sat on four knobby legs, with its pipe going up and then making an elbow to go out through the wall. To the left of the stovepipe, not far from the ceiling, a small window let in a bit of light. Along the wall on the right end of the room, four bunks stood cheek by jowl. Two more stood next to me on my right, and none of the six looked occupied. I set my gear on the closest bunk and looked at Diente Frío, who nodded and walked away.

I laid out my bedroll on top of the next cot, and I set my warbag on the floor between the two. I took off my gunbelt, which I had been wearing ever since I left Pueblo, and I stowed it in my bag. Then I went out to sit by myself in the patio and wait for Nena.

The shadows were stretching out and the air was cooling. I could hear voices inside the house, amid the clanking of kitchen utensils. From the corral area I could hear the sounds of cattle and horses, and men calling back and forth. I felt safe and relaxed inside the rancho, which was how I imagined people were expected to feel. This was a place where paunchy men were supposed to be able to smoke cigarettes and watch the bullbats chasing insects in the evening sky overhead, or a place where old widowed sisters met two or three times a year, sat and visited on plank benches, and went back to their respective ranchos. It was a place where little children chased kittens and broke piñatas while adults who stayed up drinking the night before tried to sleep late in the dark guest rooms. That was Rancho Alegre, as I was getting to know it, and I was sorry that its solid character now had the stain of having had a young man die outside the front door.

I assumed Ramón had been transported to town by now, and in the meanwhile, Don Alvino would be taking it all very gravely. I could picture him sitting around a table with his remaining preferred guests, Webb Finley among them and clucking out a bit of wisdom now and then. I thought it was just as well that I sat out here in my cane-bottom chair rather than stand inside and be cross-examined.

After a while Nena came out, carrying a plate that looked promising. As she came closer, I saw a fair serving of the same kind of meat and beans I had eaten the day before. The food was steaming, so I imagined it was all right. Nena handed me the plate, then pulled a chair close to me and sat down.

"And how is everyone inside?" I asked.

"Oh, fine. They're having supper."

"That's good." I dug into my own food.

"It gives Don Alvino much pain that there should be a death here, of that kind, especially when he is having a fiesta."

"I'm sure. And have they taken Ramón to town?"

"Early this morning. César was gone almost all day."

"And the American?"

"He has not gone very far from the table. They talk for hours, and then another meal is served."

I took another spoonful myself and tried not to feel guilty. "And you and Rosa Linda? Are you enjoying yourselves?"

"Somewhat, with the visit. But we will be glad to go tomorrow. Do you go with us?"

"That's my plan. For that reason I came back to the rancho. And to see you, of course."

She smiled. "Of course. But I didn't want to take anything for granted. I know you have been busy, and I didn't know if you had more work to do."

"I think I have accomplished as much as I can on this trip. I wish I had something more definite, but I don't think I'm going to find it now."

"Well, I'm sure you did the best you could."

I had a vision of myself sitting in the street, starry-eyed and empty-handed, with an old man looking down at me. "So-so, to tell you the truth."

"There's always more work," she said, smiling again. "Maybe your next job will be better."

"I hope so. For right now, I just need to finish this one."

"Go ahead and eat," she said. "I'm making you talk too much. I'm sorry there isn't any beer."

"It's all right. I don't need any." Then I added, "But I never turn it down."

She laughed. "That's good. Maybe I'll join you for a drink when we get to Colorado Esprín."

Not long after that, when I had finished my plate, she said she had to go in. She wished me a good rest and dreams with the angels, and then she took the plate and spoon to the kitchen. As I watched her walk away, I wished she could have stayed out longer. I had a vivid memory of our one good kiss, and I thought this whole business with Ramón was delaying the next one.

I sat for a while in the patio as the dusk gathered. No one came through the courtyard, so I imagined the working men and boys took their meals in their quarters, which lay out back near the corrals. I could still hear voices from the kitchen, but no one came outside. Before long, I supposed, someone would come out to toss the dishwater, and it would be better if I wasn't sitting alone in the dark like the ghost of one of the dead young men. So I got up, went to water a flower, and found my way to the dark, heavy door of my room.

Once inside, I lit a match, but I couldn't find a lantern or a candle anywhere. I wouldn't have minded having a light for a little while, but I didn't need it badly enough to go all the way to the bunkhouse and make my request with Diente Frío. I lit another match, and finding no firewood or kindling, I decided I wasn't even going to have a blaze. So I pulled off my boots, put my hat on the other bunk, and crawled into my bedding. I told myself the rancho was a nice place, except when things got stringent with the girls.

I awoke before dawn when the roosters started crowing. The small window high on the wall showed a patch of sky that was just a little less dark than the inside of the room.

No one had come into the room during the night; I was sure of that, for I would have heard the door scraping on the floor. I had had a light sleep but a restful one, having had the place to myself, and now I was wide awake. I didn't want to get up and go out too soon, or someone might take me for a predawn prowler, so I stayed under the covers for a while and thought about the trip ahead.

I was assuming Don Alvino would send the girls to Florence in a coach, and from there they would pay for passage to Colorado Springs. My horse would be well fed and rested, and I should be able to ride along without any trouble. Beyond that broad outline, I didn't have a detailed picture of how the trip would go. But the idea of traveling with the two girls picked up my spirits, and I decided I would not worry too much about Mr. Tull until I left Colorado Springs.

When the first gray light began to show at the top of the door, I rolled out of bed. Wondering how many spiders I might have shared the room with, I thumped my hat and shook out my boots before putting them on.

I washed my hands and face at a pump in the yard. I saw a light in the kitchen, and I could smell wood smoke coming from the stovepipe. From the other side of the compound I could hear the sounds of ranch hands and animals—the call of voices, the clang of feed buckets, the thump of hooves on corral planks.

I carried a chair from the patio closer to the door of my room. Then, with the door open, I found the bit chains in my saddlebag and brought them outside with the bridle and reins. As the sun came up and the rest of the rancho stirred awake, I put on the chains and set the reins back from the bit about nine inches on each side. That should make it easier to handle the reins for the rest of the trip—or for as long as I had the horse, for that matter.

I went inside and got my gear ready, then came out to sit in the chair some more. It occurred to me to go check on my horse, so I walked around to the corrals and saw him with his nose in a pile of oats. None of the workers were around, so I guessed they had done their chores and were having breakfast. I went back to my chair.

Quite a while passed without anyone coming out of the house. The adobe walls were so thick that I couldn't hear much with the door and windows closed, but I could tell that people were up and about. I told myself to be patient and to take the day as it came.

About an hour after sunrise, Magdalena came out of the house with a tin plate of fried potatoes and an enamel cup full of coffee.

"I thought you would be up by now," she said. "Everyone is getting ready, and we should be leaving in a while."

"That's good," I said. "There's no hurry."

She went inside, and I had my breakfast without ceremony. I thought Magdalena had been brief, but I wasn't going to worry about things ahead of time.

At about the time I finished my breakfast, I heard noise at the big door. I walked a few steps toward the courtyard so I could see, and there were two boys pushing open the big hinged halves of the *portón*. Outside the doorway was the rear end of a coach, which began moving backward in small jerks. From the driver's seat came a voice that sounded like the nasal tones of Diente Frío.

It took him a full ten minutes to get the coach backed into the *portal,* with much hollering at the horses and scolding at the two boys as he jacked the coach one way or the other, pulled it forward, and tried again. At last he got it situated outside the kitchen door, so he set the brake, got down, and opened the doors.

There followed about twenty minutes of bustle, during which time Diente Frío and another *chalán* carried out bandboxes, valises, and handbags, set them up on top, re-arranged them, put some of the smaller articles inside the coach, brought out more bags, transferred some things from inside to the top again, and generally made a big production of loading a moderate amount of baggage. Toward the end of the work, Webb Finley came out wearing his bicyclist's cap and brandishing a traveler's stick. He gave orders to Diente Frío and the other man, told the boys to stay out of the way, and kept his back to me the whole time.

I was wondering what to make of the whole spectacle when Magdalena came out to speak with me.

"Is everyone traveling together in the same coach?" I asked. I was careful to use *diligencia* as they did at the rancho, and not *carruaje* as I heard Finley say.

"So it seems." She had an uncomfortable look about her.

"Is there something wrong?"

"Well, things have changed somewhat." After shooting a glance at Webb Finley, who still had his back to us, she said, "The large American has been speaking a great deal with Don Alvino, who thinks we should go through Pueblo. Because of the danger. That way, we all go in the same coach, and the man will see us to the train station."

"The train station?" I had the feeling that Magdalena was being pulled away from my reach.

"Yes. And he has not said it yet, but I fear that he presumes to go on the train with us to Colorado Esprín." She flicked her eyes his way again, then said, with clear displeasure, "We do not need him. We do not even need to go to Pueblo."

"Can't you just say you'll do it the way you want?"

"You know how the people are. Doña Elena is Rosa Linda's aunt, and Don Alvino gives the orders here. When we get to Pueblo, it will be different."

"Well, that should not be difficult. But if you are going to go on the train, I don't know how I can travel with you. Of course, I can ride as far as Pueblo with you."

Now she had a crestfallen look. "This is a bad thing to say," she began, "and it is not my idea. But Don Alvino says he doesn't think the young gringo is a good person to go along with a widow and two young girls. Because your relation to the dead young man and his friend, also dead, is not clear."

I let it sink in. That was why I got tended to the way I did, and not necessarily because of anything I did. "I see. In the end, the old gringo doesn't want me to go along, as he wants to be the gallant one. And he has convinced Don Alvino."

Her expression was clearing up, but she still seemed dejected. "So it seems. I am very sorry, and I am glad you are not angry with me. I did not know the full of it until this morning."

"Of course I'm not angry with you. But let's decide one thing. Do you want me to go to Pueblo, on the chance that we might travel together from there? I can ride along behind the coach and not bother anyone."

"Why not?" Her eyes softened. "Rosa Linda does not like him, either, and we will get rid of him there. But here at the rancho, we can not say much, with Don Alvino."

"I understand." I looked toward the coach, where Diente

Frío and his helper were pulling a sheet of canvas over the baggage on top. "It looks as if it's time for me to get my horse ready, then," I said.

"César says it is tied in front."

That burned me as much as anything. They wanted to play here's-your-hat-and-what's-your-hurry, but nobody wanted to be the one to tell me, so they shoved it off on her. "Don't worry," I said, looking her in the eyes. "Everything will be fine when we get to Pueblo." I made a kissing motion with my lips, and she did the same. Then she turned and walked back to the house. Webb Finley must have known I was watching, for he didn't look her way at all as he pointed at the canvas with his stick.

I hauled my gear out front, and one of the boys came to watch.

"He's a big horse. He eats all the grain from the other horses."

"That's good. Did he drink water, too?"

"Oh, yes."

I put on a leather glove and started rubbing down the horse with the flat of my hand.

"César says you know who killed the young man, and for that reason you don't go with the girls."

"César knows more than I do. So does the fat American, and he is riding inside the coach with the girls, isn't he?"

"Yes, but he has a horse. César says they will tie it behind."

"Huh."

I made short work of saddling my horse and tying on my gear. As I did so, I could hear the women saying their good-byes inside the *portal*. When I had everything snug,

I walked my horse out about forty yards from the entrance and waited.

Diente Frío came shuffling from the corrals with a large blue roan on the end of a lead rope. The horse was saddled, and it looked as if it was going to tag along as the boy said. Diente Frío tied the horse to the hitch rail, climbed up onto the driver's seat, pulled the coach out of the entryway, untied the horse, and snugged the lead rope to a ring on the back of the vehicle. Then, with a final round of farewells, louder now, the women came out into the sunlight and climbed into the coach. Webb Finley handed each of them in and then hauled himself up and inside, pulling his stick in with him and then reaching back for the door. Diente Frío shook the reins and hollered a command, and the coach pulled away.

Three women came out waving handkerchiefs and calling more good-byes and God-bless-yous. Then they went in, and the two boys pushed the big halves of the door closed. I let the coach get a quarter-mile start on me, and then I put my spurs to the horse and left Rancho Alegre behind.

Chapter Fifteen

The coach moved at such a slow pace that I wondered how long it would take to get to Pueblo. Diente Frío kept the horses reined in, and he poked along as if he were in a funeral procession. Even at a casual walk, my horse kept catching up. At moments I would hear laughter coming out of the open windows of the coach, and I resented the image I had of the large American holding forth with all his wit in Spanish. When I got that close, Diente Frío would turn to me, scowl, and wave me back. Then I would lag until the coach pulled well ahead, and whenever it turned a little to the right, I could see the knob of Webb Finley's traveling stick poking out the window on his side.

We couldn't have been going any more than four miles an hour. When the sun had risen high in the east, I could still see the rancho, small patches of white in a grove of cottonwoods. At midmorning I saw a rider watching us from a hill on the south, and I tried to pay him no mind until I saw him waving at the coach. Then I saw that it was Felipe, and I waved at him. He waved back.

The morning warmed, and time dragged on. Dust rose

from the wheels of the coach and from the hooves of the blue roan. I found myself gazing off in the distance and seeing nothing but a haze of hills and trees. For a while I watched a hawk overhead, until my horse spooked and I almost took a dive. I saw a twisted stick, a stray piece of sagebrush, that he must have taken for a snake.

The sun had crossed its high point when we came to the first big draw. I knew we were over halfway to Pueblo then. Diente Frío eased the coach, rocking and swaying, down into the bottom and then let the horses take the uphill grade on a steady pull. The next draw was wider, nearly three hundred yards across at the bottom, so when I came to a level spot I stopped my horse to let the coach creep ahead.

I was watching the wheels turn and the blue roan plod along when all of a sudden my horse made a big lurch upward and forward. Then I heard the crash of a rifle, and I knew someone had taken aim at me from somewhere on the left. My horse let out a loud, wheezing squeal and plunged forward at a dead run. He had almost caught up to the coach, where the blue roan was sidestepping, when he began to lose his footing. *This is it,* I thought, and I kicked my stirrups loose. I heard another shot, but I think it cut the air behind me. Then my horse collapsed, and I went tumbling off to the right as another shot kicked up dirt in front of me.

The coach had taken off at a dash. It looked as if Diente Frío had reined in the horses at the first shot but they got spooked with the second and third, and they were off and running. I scrambled back to take cover behind my horse, which was as still as any dead thing. As I dove behind the broad body, I realized that my rifle was on the up side if I dared to reach for it. Hunkered down alongside my dead horse, I couldn't see anything in the direction the shots had come from, but I could see the coach bouncing and swaying as it careened off the trail and into the washed-out bottom of the draw. Then it came to a stop, still upright, and the blue roan tumbled. I could hear Diente Frío shouting at the team as the coach jerked but did not move forward. The roan came up onto its feet, and a door opened on the right side of the coach.

Now I dared to peek up over the withers of my horse. I saw a clump of rocks on the side of the draw I had just ridden down, and I figured that was where the shots had come from. Whoever had fired had me pretty well pinned down, but they couldn't come and get me without being seen by the people in the coach. I looked over at the blue roan, about two hundred yards away, and I thought how useful he would be if he wasn't so far.

Then I looked back at the rocks. I thought I saw movement and a glint of sunlight on metal, so I ducked. When I peeked up again, I saw a rider coming out from a bend in the draw. It looked like Matthew Tull, and he was leading another horse. A bulky, dark-hatted figure who could have been no one but Hibbard sprang up from the rocks, carrying a rifle, and ran toward the horses. It was an odd-looking rifle, thicker than most, and I thought it must have a long telescopic sight on it. Hibbard grabbed the set of reins Tull handed him, and the horse danced around as the man tried to poke the rifle into the scabbard. Failing that, he tried to mount up with the rifle in his hand, and he dropped it on the off side of his horse. Then he and Tull turned their horses and headed for the other side of the draw.

I had changed my way of thinking about Hibbard, and

pretty damn quick. Anyone who takes shots at me with a rifle isn't just bullying around. And the man Hibbard was working for was just as much to blame. I reached over the shoulder of my horse, pulled my rifle from its scabbard, and settled back to get an aim across the swells of my saddle. I levered in a shot, snickety-snick. I didn't care which of the two men I hit, but I knew I needed to try. I picked up Hibbard, who was on this side of the two and made a good target. I drew a bead on him as the horses started to climb the slope. It was a long shot, but when it seemed like things came together, I fired.

Damned if I didn't miss Hibbard and his horse both, but hit Matthew Tull's horse, which was on the other side of them and just uphill. The horse took a spill, and Tull rolled clear. He called to Hibbard, who turned around and came down the slope. I thought, *They'd like to get their hands on that blue roan, too.*

Tull was standing now, bareheaded, barking some kind of orders at Hibbard, who had pulled to a stop. Tull grabbed the rein of the horse, down by the bit, and Hibbard was trying to back the horse away from him. Tull pulled at Hibbard's arm, and the big man slapped back. Then Tull drew his pistol, took aim, and shot Hibbard at close range. Hibbard fell back and off the right side, and the horse almost trampled Tull, but he held on to the reins and got the animal pulled around straight. With the pistol still in his hand, he swung up into the saddle.

The horse stood still as Tull gathered his reins. I could see the hatless blond head and the white shirt above the dark vest. I forgot about the rest of the world as I aimed at the white spot. Everything seemed to come together again, and I squeezed the trigger.

I could tell I hit him dead center from the way he pitched forward and tumbled headfirst to the ground. The horse bolted away, up and over the hill, in a matter of seconds.

I looked across to my right to see how the coach was getting along. It had quit jostling, and Diente Frío was peeking around the hind end. Webb Finley was helping Doña Elena down from the step.

With my rifle in hand, I walked across the draw. I was taking no chances after what I had just been through and seen. But everything was still—Tull's horse, Hibbard, and Tull himself. I walked to within five yards of him where he lay with his watch chain glinting in the sunlight. Then I thought of Lawrence Tull's words: "Please find my son for me if you can."

I stood there for a long minute until movement caught my eye. Webb Finley was angling up the slope, stabbing at the ground with his traveling stick. I waited for him to come up next to me and lift his chin toward the dead man.

"Matthew Tull," I said.

Finley gave a slow nod. "That's the virtuous son, all right."

I shook my head, thinking about everything that had gone to waste. "It seems as if he had a lot to hide."

"More than meets the eye. From what I've heard, there are others in Pueblo who could tell you the color of his ink." Finley stretched his face down and then relaxed it. "But it looks like he's out of options."

At the train station in Pueblo, Diente Frío handed down my saddle and gear and then went to untying the canvas that covered the baggage. He had not spoken to me all the rest of the way, even though I had sat next to him on the driver's seat. As I stood on the ground, I watched Webb Finley help the two girls out of the coach. He did not look at me or talk to me, but he chatted with Diente Frío as the two of them took down the bags and boxes for the young ladies.

When the coach rolled away with the blue roan following, Magdalena said, "I think he is very unhappy, the American."

"Let him be."

"He said you put us in danger, just as he told Don Alvino. It was all your fault."

"I suppose it was, but it took no skin off his nose. Nobody shot at him. But I lost a horse, and I can't expect to be paid for the rest of my work. Not the way things turned out."

"But you will still do a report to the old man?"

"I can write him. There will be time on the train."

Her face brightened. "Oh, that's good. Then you won't be in a hurry to go back."

"No hurry at all. When we get to Espreen, I would like to find a place to take a bath. After that, I would like to go someplace where nobody knows me. Have a steak hot from the fire, a cold beer, and charming company."

"You have good ideas," she said. "I know where all of those things can be done."